The Names of the Lost

The Names of the Lost

Liza Wieland

Southern Methodist University Press
Dallas

This novel is a work of fiction. Names, characters, places,
and incidents are either the product of the author's
imagination or are used fictitiously. Any resemblance to
actual events, locales, or persons, living or dead, is entirely
coincidental.

First edition, 1992

Requests for permission to reproduce material from this work
should be sent to:
    Permissions
    Southern Methodist University Press
    Box 415
    Dallas, Texas 75275

Library of Congress Cataloging-in-Publication Data

Wieland, Liza.
    The names of the lost / Liza Wieland. — 1st ed.
       p.   cm.
    ISBN 0-87074-337-6 (hardcover)
    I. Title.
    PS3573.I344N3   1992
    813'.54—dc20   92-53614

Design by Whitehead & Whitehead

To my family,
and for the children

When you grip
my arm and lean way out
and shout out the holy names
of the lost neither of us is scared
and our tears mean nothing.

Philip Levine

GIRLS *always like to go swimming at night. If it's late enough in the evening, they don't have to wear bathing suits, and no matter what month of summer, the water always feels like it's got oil floating on top and fixing to mark them the way paint would. When they come back inside, no one will have to ask where they've been. One look and everybody will know the truth. The night air is thick and sweet the way their mothers smell, like the earth laid open and dark. To walk outside now is to be blinded and even the slow flash of heat lightning is no use when they need to see where they are.*

It's dangerous to swim like this but that's why they do it. There's nights it gets so still, every girl will raise her head out of the water and wonder if she hasn't been left behind, if she isn't really alone in this world. If you're with them and you stop moving to come up for air, you can hear their breathing and see their heads clearing the water's surface like moonrise. Or else they might look to you like some of the darker planets casting their shadows over the earth. You feel like drowning and you know these girls are the only ones who can save you. A pool in summer is a fifth element, it's like space, and girls know you can only breathe in it if they teach you how. Without them it would be so easy to sink to the bottom, to be taken by the water's dark arms and lost forever.

The girls I know would do it this way: Gus will get here first and wait with her feet in the water at the shallow end until Noreen comes out of the house with a citronella candle. She'll put it down on the step next to Gus and they'll keep waiting, their faces strangely twinned by the small orange fire. Finally Robbie Lynn will appear at the gate, a piece of the darkness moving in closer. There's nights when they'll all three swim for hours and go home without a single word spoken between them. It gets that way with people who are almost family but not quite. It gets to be that you have to reel them out some so you can reel them in again.

They've known each other a long time, nine years since this pool was dug in the garden behind Noreen Gresham's house. Back then it was another summer of waiting like all summers are, and when they couldn't stand it any longer, they climbed up on the rented backhoe and slid down into the raw earth where the swimming pool would be. They wrote their names on the cool dirt walls, climbed out, and watched while Willis Gresham poured in the aggregate and lime. They asked questions about depth and the gallons of water needed to fill until Mr. Gresham told them to go back to their work.

They were at the end of grade school and had jobs mowing lawns and babysitting. They got to like mowing lawns because they were too young to see the danger in it. A boy they knew had lost two fingers in his daddy's lawnmower, but secretly these girls loved the satiny ridge on his hand where the fingers should be, and they thought of holding that hand in movie theaters or in crowded places where no one else would know. And then they got to like the way people would try to talk at them over the noise of the engine, and they would pretend not to understand even if they could. The growl of the mower always stayed in their heads for a long time afterwards. It grew to become a huge animal chasing them all night just under the surface of their dreams.

But the very day this pool was squared, the cement walls set and ready to be filled, they ran away together. All three of them packed small suitcases and walked four blocks up Peachtree Battle, over Woodward Way, and then across Northside Drive to the golf course. They were gone all afternoon, missed supper, and still hadn't turned up by dark.

It was Noreen's brother Ray who went looking and found them. He went because he loved Robbie Lynn back then just the way he does now. He stood high on a hill near Sagamore and watched them racing up and down in the creekbed, keeping perfectly quiet so that the only sounds were splashing water, their breathing, and farther away, the swish of sprinklers on the greens. Their suitcases were lying open by the creekbank, waiting to be unpacked into the air.

Two old men out walking stopped next to Ray and whistled low. It must be a vision, they said, meaning this clear night in July, the whole expanse of fairway shining crisp and silvery and breathless.

Truly, one said.

Verily, the other said.

It's like they're not even real, another voice said behind them, another man out walking in the dark.

There was something clean and animal about them, sharp and just barely graceful, still wild.

When they run, Ray said, they remind me of horses.

Colts, said the first two beside him, new in this world.

Their eyes are like swords, said the third, they can cut through darkness.

In this same town, named Atlanta, children disappear. For a year now, they've been taken from back yards and playgrounds, curbsides and parking lots, their bodies left to rot in the woods or drift along down the Chattahoochee River, deeper and deeper into the water's long wound. In whispers you'll hear of another one missing, you'll see lists of their names, first, middle, and last, ringing out from the evening paper. You'll see their pictures in the grainy newsprint, their parents and brothers and sisters, heads bent, trying to turn away from the camera.

You'll hear them tonight, singing up out of the kudzu, singing high and lonesome in this Georgia darkness, crying for their

3

mommas. *Their voices mingle and the refrain of that song comes over and over, all night long rising ghostly out of your lawns and hedges, as they become mist off your bodies of water. In the morning, your grass is trampled and their tears are everywhere.*

Now in the woods surrounding the pool, the crickets and peepers sound rusty, parts of a child's toy moving too fast. Everyone in this city feels it, little wounds opening in their hearts and getting bigger every day. Everybody hears it, the voices of invisible children murmuring deep in the woods, calling you to come find them. Quick, they say. Now.

Noreen

GOD love her and all, but Robbie Lynn is what you call a bolter. I've told her that's what she is but she says she can't help it. When anything bothers her, she runs, or nowadays, she gets in a car and drives. Me, I stick around because I can't move. Time slows down to a crawl, I get rooted to the spot, just like they say, and can't tear my eyes away from whatever sight it is Robbie can't bear. The only time Robbie didn't run and I did was the day we found the boy in the river. She hung there with her body swaying half out of the water making choking sounds. I was the one took off up the riverbank and when I looked back it was like the three of them in a picture, Gus, Robbie, and the boy they were trying to carry up onto the sand.

What made me take off like that was seeing his face, just a flash of it before they got to him. If you've ever seen a drowned person, you know how it stays with you. They get discolored and fat with the water inside them and they don't look human. You go around for days trying to puzzle out how a body could come to look that way, and it gets to be like that body is right there beside you, risen and walking and won't rest until you explain how it got to be so ugly.

That day, though, when I got to the top of the bank, I had at least a quarter mile back to the car, which I must have run, then ten minutes down to Westmoreland's Gulf station at the end of the road. I told Westmoreland what we found and he called the police from his office. Everybody kept asking questions, but alls I could say was *Jesus Jesus* and try to remember the

Act of Contrition. I had got as far as Oh my God I am heartily sorry when somebody brought me a Coke and I took it but I felt like I had to get back. I was starting to feel bad for running off that way. It wasn't how we ever did things, me and Gus and Robbie. I never even opened that Coke, just carried it in the car and clear over to the edge of the bank where I could see down to that same still life of Gus and Robbie Lynn and the drowned boy.

A police cruiser had already pulled in off the road. When I got down to the river Robbie was sitting on the ground with her back to me, and Gus was doing all the work, describing to the officers how we first saw him and calling herself Augusta and Robbie Lynn, Roberta. Her voice had a kind of clutch to it, like she'd just spit out a penny. By the end of the questions, six more policemen and two ambulance drivers had come hiking down to us. They walked up the riverbank in both directions, then wrapped the body in canvas and hauled it up to the road and out of sight.

When they finally let us go we had an escort looking already like a funeral parade back to Westmoreland's and then the cruisers turned right toward town and we were on our own. I pulled into the alley that runs along behind Northside Drive and we just sat. I closed my eyes and leaned my head back. The taste of rotten milk rose up in the back of my mouth. Gus turned on the radio then flipped it right off so alls we heard was the announcer's voice wishing us a good afternoon.

"I don't want to go home," Gus said.

"Me neither," Robbie said.

Nobody would be at my house. We left the car clicking and hissing in the garage and went straight upstairs to take showers in Momma and Daddy's bathroom, just to be rid of the river smell, and went back outside to the pool, staying in the water until it got dark. Then we took off our suits and kept swimming, only it was more like drifting, maybe even sleeping, and hours passed and we didn't know. Robbie said it's funny how there's no place this water couldn't touch us, then she stayed quiet until Ray came home and they moved off into the deep end, treading water and whispering to each other.

Now it's the next morning and Momma is fixing us breakfast. She got home late and asked if Daddy was back and when we told her no she went upstairs without saying anything else. I think I can see the sharp points of her shoulder blades moving like real knives under her bathrobe while she butters the toast. Gus is reading out loud about us from the front page of the paper, *three swimmers* it said, making me feel holy in a way I don't deserve.

Elijah

AFTER the service his momma offer to give me some of his things, but I don't want none of it. She say because we was such good of friends and having it all in her house got to be bad enough all that time he was missing, but now it be like even the sight of his shoes is more than she can stand. His shoes lay there by his bed saying you all ain't walked far enough to find me and his clothes, even what he hadn't been wearing for weeks, they all stinks like the river they pull him out of. Ain't no amount of washing can make it go away, she tell my momma. It like to be in this whole house. So she carried everything outside and set fire to it and she say to my momma she wished that fire would take her house and her along with it.

Robbie Lynn

THAT boy dead in the river is still following us and making trouble with his swelled-up fingers, then stepping back and looking at what he's done out of his round black eyes. Two more boys from the south side turn up missing, then Ray's and Noreen's father disappears too. He tells their mother he's flying up to Chattanooga on business, and he never comes home. She says she knew what he had in mind because of some of the things he took with him, but when Ray asks what she shakes her head and won't tell. She reports him missing, but there's nothing to go on. He didn't even take the car.

Whole days, Noreen lays on her bed, not crying, not doing anything she says except trying to fix him in her head while she still can. I tell her to put a lit candle in the window at night. I tell her the real name for citronella is lemon balm, and she likes the sound of that, cool and steady and just what you need. One part of me knows her daddy's far away by now. The other part, what I would call sixth sense and fourth dimension, it's thinking he might see that candle, take it for a sign and come on back.

Ray though, he's started driving around the city looking for his daddy. Every day he'll pick a different part of town and go over it street by street. He tells me when he sees a man who's about six foot tall with blonde hair, he'll stop the car, get out, and follow him until he's sure it's not who he's looking for. Twice he's lost his track and had to start all over in the same place the next day. He doesn't talk to anybody or cause trouble, except by double-parking downtown late in the afternoon, but when he has to do that, he leaves the motor running. He checks the mailbox every few hours and reads the personal ads in all the papers. He says his daddy wouldn't have gone very far, or else he's left a message that only Ray would understand. One night he was up late telling me all this, and I asked what he'd do if one day he found his daddy, maybe walking along a street or buying groceries in a store. Ray looked at me like I'd just asked him his own name and I said I know, you'd bring him back. Maybe you'd even kill him if that was the only way. Isn't that right, Ray, I said, moving closer to him on the sofa and running my hand high up on his leg, isn't that right?

Gus

"SHOOT, Gus," Noreen said, "how do you do those tears that way? You're Academy Award material if I ever saw it."

"It was real tears," I said. "You try calling up your grandma and telling her you just drove her car off Fox Mountain and see if you don't cry some too."

That was yesterday, Billy, after I misjudged a little rise off Stillhouse Road up in back of school. So I guess you could say I'm in trouble again, but you know I'm beginning to think it's a curse on me, Grandma always says so anyways, you got the curse of my name, Augusta Grace Searing. The curse of working dance halls, wearing false eyelashes and cheating at cards. Some of me must have rubbed off, she says, since you been living here nigh to forever and further back than that, ever since your crazy momma rung my front doorbell, handed you over, and walked off into the night without a thought for anybody but her own self.

She says to watch out or else I'll grow up to be a drifter or a carney, but you know, I think I'm already headed down that road. I still do admire Robbie and Noreen and the way they can live alongside the rest of the world. But like you would always say, I have to decide things and take charge and I happen to think it's a pretty good way to be. Make decisions, good or bad, but make them. You used to say that too and so now I say it because I love you probably way too much even after all this time and I like the idea of using the words you did. It's being made over in your image.

Grandma says honey it's the story of this life, people die and you don't even get to say a word to them, not good-bye or nothing. Look at your own sorry momma, she says. Look at those little boys on the south side. She hooks a Pall Mall in her mouth, shuffles and deals. She's teaching me how to play rummy so I can go with her on Friday nights. She says cards'll give me something to do in college too.

I've been going with her to Partelle's most Fridays since my arm got broke because she thinks I need watching. They let me drink a beer and listen in on their conversations and sometimes they ask what I think, but I don't usually say. Mrs. Partelle used to teach one of the missing boys in Sunday school and she can't talk about anything else. It kind of makes you sick inside, the way people always like to brag about being close to tragedy like they're hungry for sorrow they think they won't ever get in this world.

I have to admit it though, I can't help listening, and then a week ago I was thinking about you and out of the blue I started a list of those missing children's names. Next to the names I write their ages, where they lived and their mommas' and daddys' names and whether they've been found yet. But you know, it's not just me, everybody's been paying attention to them. You can't see a kid now without watching after him until he turns a corner or opens a door and goes inside and even then you have to hold yourself back from following.

There's come to be a quiet in town that gets ahold of everybody these days. In May you know how the night air isn't so filled up with crickets and bats and starlings crying in their sleep, so you notice sounds, where they come from and how long they last. You count them out in your head, against the time of your heartbeats. You hear the differences in kids' mothers' voices calling them home. I can hear Skiff and Ellie Wager next door doing wheelies on their spyder bikes, hear their voices catch in their throats as they pull up on the handlebars, and the *plomp* of the front tires as they touch down. It's the same noise all your muscles make when they finally ease up and let you go to sleep. It sounds like a body falling overboard, or now that I think of it, your armbone breaking in two, the way it's muffled under those seven layers of skin.

It's still only Noreen and Ray that know the true story of how I broke mine. Grandma thinks I took a spill in the dark, which is partway true. The whole truth is it was Robbie Lynn's idea, but I don't blame her much. She wanted us to kidnap her from her own birthday party, and I for one couldn't think of any good reason not to. Ray was just home from that school his daddy's sending him to up in Vermont, so she wanted to be with just him and Noreen and me.

She was already waiting for us when we drove up, and Billy, you should have seen her, standing down by her mailbox in a white dress and holding a pair of high-heeled pumps. Her feet and legs were bare. She always says she can't see the point of stockings and it seemed dangerous even to have yourself bound up like that. What if you had to make a fast getaway?

Noreen rolled down the window and when Robbie leaned in, her necklace of tiny white shells drifted against the glass like they were in an aquarium. Their color picked up what was left of the daylight and threw it toward her face. You stare at her and you can see that from having her picture taken all the time, she knows how to behave in different kinds of light, how to pitch her body toward you and become irresistible.

"Can I convince you to kidnap me?" she asked us.

"Sure," I said.

"But Robbie," Noreen said, "won't they miss you at your own birthday?"

"Maybe maybe not."

A car was easing toward us, checking house numbers.

"Let's go," I said. "Now or never."

Robbie Lynn opened the door behind Noreen and climbed in back with Ray.

"Noreen," he said, moving his face close to Robbie Lynn's shoulder, his eyes caught on her necklace, "how much gas do we have?"

He still talks to Robbie that way, seeming to converse with the rest of us but always looking at her, his eyes having nothing to do with the words coming out of his mouth. His eyes keep her out of the conversation, keep her all to himself. It's like he wants to take her thoughts and her words, maybe even take Robbie's breath and hold it for her.

"Enough," Noreen said. "Robbie, how did you get away?"

"I'm not sure," she said, looking back at Ray like he knew the answer.

She didn't say another word until we were out on Lindbergh and into a pitch-dark bar called The Twenty-Seven Birds. We sat down and ordered beers from a waitress we could barely see except for the white collar on her shirt and the flash of her earrings where they caught the red light from the exit sign. It was just her voice saying yes two times, once like a question and once like its own answer. You get to thinking a place like this must be full of runaways and missing persons and secret rendezvous. You get to thinking if you turned on the lights, you might really find out something worth knowing.

"How I got away is when people started to arrive," Robbie Lynn said, as if we were still back at her house and had just then asked the question, "I told my father I wasn't ready yet, and when it sounded like there was enough of a crowd, I walked out the back door and down through the graveyard."

We didn't talk about it anymore. Instead, we thought we might try to drink as many beers as there were seagulls and sandpipers on the sign outside.

"We were decorating the yard this morning," Robbie Lynn said, then stopped and shook her head. "Mother's got a new idea for the peach trees, I mean for keeping the squirrels away. Really it's two ideas going on at once. First, she's got pie plates made out of tinfoil to hang up. They catch the sun and when the wind knocks them together it makes a sizzling noise, which they think is a snake. Then she hangs snakes in the branches."

"Real snakes?" Noreen said.

"Real plastic snakes, from Woolworth's. Mostly cobras with those flexible wire spines."

"I'd shoot them," Ray said, but we knew it was just big talk for Robbie Lynn to hear.

"She wanted to put them up in time for the party," Robbie Lynn said. "Don't you think that's strange?"

I remember none of us said a word. Her birthday seemed already over with, and sad.

When we got back to Robbie Lynn's house that night, it was after eleven, but cars were still parked up and down the street. Above us, her yard was shot with light from outdoor lanterns. I looked for the huge dripping shadows of snakes in the peach trees, but they were hard to see. It was warm for early April and we could hear the quavering voices of guests who'd come outside to stand in the night air, smoking and maybe wandering off into the woods as guests will always do.

We stopped to listen and then Noreen pulled on into the Wilkinses' driveway, where we got out and started to walk up through the graveyard. Last year the Atlanta Historical Society finally came and dug up most of the Civil War coffins, and they've filled in the graves, but the new earth has sunk two feet in some places, so you know just what you're walking over. Some of the markers are still left but even in daylight you can barely see them, they're so covered with moss. We played there when we were kids, way before I knew you, then one day we made a campfire that spread and burned out a lot of the ground cover. We didn't go back after that. No one ever told us to stay away, we just did.

"Don't come up," Robbie Lynn said. "There might be a scene."

I myself didn't think there would be any scene. None of the hundred and something guests believed they'd see all that much of Robbie Lynn anyways, and when she came walking up out of the graveyard in that dress and her white skin, you wouldn't expect yelling and screaming. Nobody could possibly have found any words for what they saw before their very eyes.

We kept lookout from behind the headstones, and we watched a woman drop her glass with a little cry. Robbie just smiled and said she'd get the broom and walked past them all into the house. Noreen started laughing and then she couldn't help herself and had to sit down on the ground. Her breath came jolting out of her in heaves and sighs.

By then Robbie Lynn and her father had come outside to stand under the porch light, and he was talking to her in a low voice, his body taut and swayed back a little, held away from her on purpose. She had one hand on her hip and the other raised high over her head, supporting her weight against the screen door. Her father looked up when Noreen laughed again, glanced back at Robbie Lynn and then started walking down the hill toward us. He had to take his hands out of his pockets and hold them out for balance over the sunken ground.

"Who's there?" Mr. Wilkins said. Then he called back over his shoulder, "Robbie, who was with you?"

She leaned full against the screen door with her eyes closed, smiling. Once she raised her hand to wave in our direction.

"Gus Searing is that you?" her father said.

"No," I called back.

I heard Noreen pull in her breath, then she and Ray took off down the hill towards the car. I could hear them go, breaking off twigs and crunching leaves underfoot. Alls I could think to do was follow them, but I didn't get very far past a low headstone and a length of wire hedging. I tried to clear them both at the last minute and felt my body hang in the air for what seemed like eternity.

When I hit the ground, my arm made that *plomp* sound against another headstone, and I knew it was a clean fracture, even before the pain came on. The echo of it seemed to spin off through the woods, like branches breaking farther and farther away until there was complete silence. I lay there for a minute, my legs stretched out behind me on the stone, listening to Mr. Wilkins stop short behind me and waiting for that broken feeling to set in.

The cast came off last week, not a moment too soon. The afternoons were already starting to heat up and my wrist would go warm and then I could feel the sweat trickling back down to the inside of my elbow, like a million spiders crawling around between the plaster and the skin. It's crazy I know but I have a notion that this is how it would feel to be buried alive and God saw fit to give me a little taste of it before my time came.

When the doctor cut the cast away, the sight nearly made me sick, all that loose flesh hanging off the bone like an old lady's arm. It looked like it might have a mind of its own to drag me off to places I wouldn't necessarily want to go. The nurse said it would have to be watched and that struck me funny because I thought so too but in a different way. It had the look of something small and dangerous you might start to underestimate.

To celebrate the first of June, we went swimming, me and Robbie Lynn and Noreen, down in the river a mile or so from school. It's where you and I used to swim by ourselves, where the water moves fast and silent but then slows and breaks off into smaller coves. Robbie and Noreen went on ahead and I stayed back in the trees where I watched the water run past. Being there by myself I could understand the temptation to lie down on a river and let it carry you off.

I have some pills to stop what I call phantom pain, that ache where the bone all of a sudden remembers it's been broke, and they're making me feel kind of crazy, quiet one minute, then whooping and hollering that I could swim this river in one breath. I was thinking about you too but you seemed far off, at the end of a long tunnel where my voice could hardly get to. Then I was tripping myself up on the riverbank and saying we should peel off our suits and hang them in the tree branches. We

27

laughed so hard it made us fall backwards in the water to where we could see the pine trees close over us, then we turned half swimming, half wading out into the stream and around to the cove that's closest to the bridge. In there the water's waist deep and has that sticky feel to it, like it would be sweet if you bent over and lapped some up with your tongue. It moves slow, but there's whirlpools too. Not the kind that suck you down and drown you, but ones that spin slow and easy, the speed you might turn yourself if you were up on dry land.

The body was in one of those shallow whirlpools, caught face down half on a log and turning slowly like he was trying to see something under water from every possible angle. At first I thought it was a tree limb and I think if he'd been white, I'd have known it for a body right away. We tried to stop where we were, but some kind of cross current was driving us in closer to where we'd run up against him. I tried to fight to stay away, but you can't fight water like you can't fight air, and there was a place where I just gave up, stumbled on into him and stayed there with his leg resting against my shoulder.

"Noreen," I said, but she was already out of the water and halfway up the hill toward the road.

"Should I go with her?" Robbie Lynn said, letting it seem like I was in charge, even though it was too late for any of that.

"No," I told her. "You stay here and help me get him in to shore."

Past the whirlpool, the current fell away altogether and it was easier to manage, though the river bottom dipped and rose and sucked at our feet. I grabbed the extra material at the bottom of his pants leg and pulled until he was half up onto the bank. Robbie Lynn brought him around by the shoulders and turned his face to one side as she let him down onto the weeds.

We walked all the way out of the water and stood there, waiting and watching like he'd sit up any minute and we'd have to think up something polite to say. I could feel Robbie listening and hanging forward the same way I was. Then I noticed the dried blood caked around his ear, and my whole body felt hot and two curtains of darkness started to close in on either side of my face. I walked a little ways off into the ivy and leaned my bad arm on a tree. The bone gave a kind of ping just to remind me.

Even facing away like that, I knew when Robbie was about to turn him over and look. She was the only one of us who would do it. I'm not sure if it was curiosity or her way of paying respects. She'd do the same with her parents later on when they died, sit and look at their faces for a long time, even though the bones were smashed in and on top of that etched with millions of tiny cuts from the windshield.

I heard her talking and at first I couldn't make out the words. I started to tell her to be still, I didn't want to hear it, but she said it again louder. "Oh God," she said, "Gus, he's just a kid."

We stayed there like that, Robbie kneeling down by the body and me leaning against the tree until the police came. They started asking Robbie Lynn all the questions I guess because she was closest to the evidence, but she wasn't talking, and finally they listened to the answers I was giving from over beside the tree.

"Can't she talk for herself?" one of the police said to me.

"Not real well," I told him. "You probably should leave her alone."

I forgot then and went to use my arm to push away from the tree. The bone hurt like it was breaking all over again, and I swore some and held on to it.

"What's the matter?" the police said.

I told him about it being broken and I could see he was getting madder at us for being down there by ourselves in the first place. Robbie Lynn went a shade more pale and started rocking slowly on her heels, still staring down at the body. I wished Noreen would come back with the car so we could go. There was getting to be too much talk, Billy, even for me.

Billy Marsh

AT the river's edge they turn and keep walking south, past the long reach of light from the high school on the opposite bank. Noreen says they're going to be stopped by police watching on the bridges, but they call her chicken and walk on ahead, and she says I guess you're right about some things sometimes, because so far they haven't seen a single blessed soul.

Ivy vines rise up around them in tangles and clumps and run uncut down to the water, climbing high as their waists and casting the river in darkness. Close in to the bank, you can only hear the water, you can't see it unless you look farther out towards the middle. That's where it gives off its spirit, a misty white light reflecting whatever lies along the bottom out there, maybe moonstone or quartz. Or like Robbie Lynn says, albino crawdads and blonde ponies that drowned in the Gulf of Mexico a century ago and had their bleached bodies pulled five hundred miles upstream.

Gus doesn't like coming here as much as they like to, but she makes herself do it because of me. It's a swimming hole the two of us discovered last summer and in a way it breaks her up to come back but she thinks if there's any place I'm going to send her a message from the next world, it'd be here. She'll wander off by herself, then swim out to Noreen and Robbie Lynn laughing and making jokes that are more mean than funny. You forgive Gus though, because she doesn't know any other way to grieve except to act like she doesn't care. But then Robbie Lynn'll stand still and listen into the wind, whispering for them to shush, and Gus'll stop moving too and Noreen thinks she'd like to slap Robbie for carrying on that way when you can tell she hasn't heard a thing. Gus and Robbie encourage each other believing in spirits and signs and not true Jesus and heaven the way Noreen does. Most of the time they leave her behind with all their talk, and she'll feel like she has to say a long heavy prayer for their souls.

Robbie likes the river at this hour because she has what she calls night vision so it's the same as walking in daylight for her. Gus and Noreen let her lead and she'll tell them about all the sights they're missing with their mortal eyes.

Above them tonight, a car starts over the bridge, slows to a stop in the middle, and turns out its headlights. They're close enough to hear the car doors open and close, and the creak of footsteps crossing the metal spans toward the railing.

"It moves pretty fast," a man's voice says. He's nearly twenty feet above, but the water carries his voice down so it could be he's in this cove too.

"It sure sounds like it," a lady's voice says. "It sounds like you could fall in and get carried right off to who knows where and never be found."

Her voice trails away to nothing and Gus swims a little closer to the bridge to hear better, climbing up on one of the cement pilings.

"Beware," she half sings up to them, making the word drift off quavery at the end. "Keep away from here."

"Hey," the man calls, "who's down there?"

"Beware," she says again, letting go of the piling and floating under the bridge. "Beware."

The couple on the bridge whisper to each other, then get back in their car and drive off toward town.

"Gus," Noreen yells. "Gus."

For a whole minute, there's no answer, then they hear Gus splashing back toward the bridge, working hard against the current.

"Beware," she's saying, out of breath. "Robbie? Noreen? Where are you?"

"Right here," Robbie Lynn calls back to her. "I can see you, Gus. Just follow my voice."

Slap slap slap slap come Gus's tired arms on top of the water, closer now. She calls out again, just my name this time. Noreen and

34

Robbie Lynn yell back and wait to feel the little waves her swimming makes. Then her whole body runs full into them, stiff in the limbs but loose and bending through the middle.

They carry her in to shore, trying to be gentle, and she falls into the sand at their feet, breathing fast and laughing about those two she scared off the bridge. In the moonlight they are all three frightened and beautiful. Noreen and Robbie Lynn sit down beside Gus on the slick muddy bank and pretend not to wonder about the ooze of it rising up between their legs.

Noreen

DADDY'S been gone two weeks and then Robbie Lynn's parents die on the highway, and when she calls to tell me, it's just this way, without saying hello or good-bye. They were on their way back from Jonesboro in a bad rainstorm and a truck skidded into their lane. Hit them head on with a sound that most people nearby thought was thunder from the storm.

Robbie doesn't cry, or at least not that we ever see. She spends a long time at Patterson's sitting with the closed-up caskets and staring off into space. Sometimes other people come in to be with her, but with all the bodies, that little room crowds up fast. Gus and I would rather go stay with her and her brother Sam at night.

They need us then. Sam still thinks his momma and daddy are coming home and he'll fall asleep just like that in your arms, saying tell me when they get here. Robbie says her eyes hurt from watching all day, so we take turns holding a cold washcloth over them while she drifts in and out of sleep. Sometimes we'll lie down too, one on either side of her in her parents' big bed. The room is full of flowers sent by their friends. Robbie had them trucked in from Patterson's because, she said, nobody there would be able to appreciate them. The flowers are all white except for blue hydrangeas.

"There's something in the soil here," Robbie Lynn tells us. She sounds drunk, but if she is, I guess she's got the right. "Iron is what Momma always said. Too much iron. You can't ever grow the pure white ones here."

The scent of all these flowers changes every time one of us moves.

"Half of them are poisonous," she says. "Sam's not allowed to set foot in this room."

She raises her arm and points to the different arrangements.

"Belladonna lily, foxglove, narcissus, larkspur, delphinium, lily-of-the-valley. None of the others can hurt you."

We follow her hand across the room.

"They look like ghosts," Gus says.

"They do," Robbie Lynn says back.

The three of us lie there night after night, drowsing a little but mostly awake. The tall white shapes play tricks on me, seeming to come closer, more like bodies than flowers, moving toward the bed as if there's something they want to tell us before daylight can break into the room and settle everything for once and for all. In the morning we pluck out any that are withered or downright blown out and I press them in the Bible, choosing verses I know and weighting it shut with picture albums and telephone books.

I've started on nine days of prayers and fasting for the souls of the dead and departed. I'm at the end of five days now, and if I half close my eyes into the light, I can make it so there's Daddy's face hanging in the air above my closet door. Or maybe it's God's face, fixed overhead and watching me. I leave prayer cards in the pews at Our Lady of the Assumption, the message printed in big loopy girl's handwriting that won't give me away. *Say this prayer every day for nine days and you will find something that has been lost. Do not leave money as grace has no price. Do not ignore this.*

After the funeral, alls me and Robbie and Gus want to do is drive. We start for Pearson's as soon as it's dark, pick up a six-pack, and head out I-75 south toward Macon or I-85 north toward Spartanburg, depending on where we've been the night before. The first few times we talk about what Robbie Lynn has to do. Then she writes thank-you notes to everybody who sent condolences and all those white flowers, casseroles, and donations in her parents' memory.

"Do they have one memory or two?" she says.

"Why don't you say 'in memory of'?"

"Okay. Good. That's much better."

We have to pull over in lighted parking lots or highway rest areas to do the writing. I take over when she gets tired. Just before the sun comes up we eat breakfast in a Truckstops of America and drink coffee so strong it makes you tired to be that awake. Then we go home. Nobody mentions my daddy unless I do first, and I never do.

If we don't take the interstates, or if we get lost, we might end up on a two-lane road outside the city, near open land. Then we'll pull over, get out of the car, and lie down in somebody's field. We find it wakes us up some to look at the stars and try to name the constellations.

"So that's heaven," Gus says.

"Heaven," Robbie says, "heaven's too much for me."

"I just plain don't get it," Gus says. "Seems like it's a lot of mystery and not much else. Alls you got to do is say the word heaven and people start to nod real slow and stare off into space and you know alls they're thinking about is what they're going to have for supper or else getting laid."

"Gus," I say to make her be quiet.

But in my weaker moments I wonder if she isn't about right. I saw it in the Bible while I was pressing flowers, right in the middle of Corinthians. *Heaven and earth will pass away, but my words will not pass away. Prophecies will pass away, knowledge will pass away, and tongues will cease.*

Then they say they're tired of talking about heaven and Robbie asks where Gus was when it first happened, and Gus tells her the front seat of Tommy Wadell's Buick, then Gus asks and Robbie says it was in Chastain Park.

"I was thinking how it's like midnight," Gus says from out of the darkness behind me. "The first time is like midnight.

41

With midnight it's today, tomorrow, and yesterday all at the same time, for just a split second. The first time you're with a boy is the only other thing like that probably in the whole world."

"Gus," I say, "you're drunk."

"I know she is," Robbie says, "but listen to her. When you think about it, she's exactly right, it's just like midnight. One second you don't know anything, and then all of a sudden, he's right there inside and you know everything."

This is how it is with the Holy Spirit too, but I can't tell them that.

It happened to me this way last summer and I've never told anybody. I was riding a bus downtown and it was crowded. An old man was standing in the aisle, the oldest man I've ever seen, his skin gone nearly clear so you could see the blue veins traveling from his forehead up the inside of his skull. He was small and bent the way old men get, with a halo of white hair. I had a seat since I got on in Brookhaven, but he got on at the Darlington where the population count was at one million eight and I swear I saw it change right then as he showed his pass to the driver.

He stood up in front of me for five blocks. I thought everyone would rush to give him a seat but nobody did. His shoulders fell lower and lower and when I think about it now, it's a wonder nobody thought he was dying, not even me, watching him droop in the aisle that way. I wondered if he was falling asleep and then at Five Points I got up and touched him on the shoulder and that's when I saw the rosary beads in his hand. He thanked me and sat down in my seat, and I stood beside him. The air was warm where he'd left it, empty and warm, and I moved into it like it was somebody's arms.

We got off at the same spot, Butler and Peachtree, where the entrance to Underground Atlanta used to be.

"Thank you," he said. "That was right kind of you."

I smiled and didn't know what else to do. I wanted him to leave me alone and then I thought maybe I didn't.

"Just when you touched my arm," he said, "I was thinking of the Blessed Mother and the true loveliness of her face as she rose on up to heaven."

I smiled again and nodded, filled up with wonder.

"Then I turned around and Lord, it was you."

He held up his hand and made the sign of the cross over me, then walked north, the way we came on the bus. When I raised my head to look for him again, he was gone.

I saw him twice more in June and both times he acted like there was a message he was supposed to be giving to me. The last time was in the parking garage at Lenox Square and I couldn't remember where I'd put the car, and if the truth be told, if I'd even walked or rode the bus or driven or what.

I was checking up and down the aisles of cars, knowing full well he was behind me, then I stopped and squinted my eyes into the sun.

"Hidy again," he said, looking off in the same direction I was. "I guess the sun is going down fast."

"Yes," I said back. "It's sure beautiful."

"Well," he said, "things what are too beautiful can end up like to kill you." Then his voice got sweet and mighty. *Woe to you, for you are like white washed tombs, which outwardly appear beautiful, but within they are full of dead men's bones and all uncleanness. Charm is deceitful and beauty is in vain, but a woman who fears the Lord is to be praised.*

Then he made the sign of the cross over me, down across my chest and over my breasts. When I felt his hand reach down I thought I knew then, knew the truth of what he wanted all along, why he'd put himself in my path these three times and that his purpose was mortal and unclean, and I wanted to move out of his reach but it was like I'd froze there. He dropped his voice to a whisper.

Be not like a horse or a mule without understanding which must be curbed with bit and bridle else it will not keep with you.

I stepped forward to hear and his hand didn't move except

back up to make the wide open arms of the cross and didn't stay longer than it would have on his own breast. The sign was complete and it was then that I gave myself over.

Elijah

"THEY must of dragged him out right here, Elijah."

"No, Buddy," I says, "this ain't the place."

"But look, Elijah. See this track. It was something got dragged out here."

He kick off his shoes and walk out into the river.

"Come on, Elijah," he say.

Going into the river ain't ever like willful baptism no matter what anybody will tell you. It might be a real fight if you is looking to get yourself washed that way. You gots to bend from the waist to move ahead, same as if you was heading into a wind. Leaves and hunks of bark floats past against your knees, then higher up when you moves off from the bank and around a knuckle of land and on into the cove. I never have got used to the surprise of it every time a leaf or a stick catches at my middle, turns halfway around then gets carried off.

When Buddy calls my name, the sound of it come back to us, up the river, across and down again. First Buddy bend his knees and go under, then I goes, waiting till he disappear, then one more heartbeat to be alone with all them stars and the suck of that river coming into her banks. Then I drop down too till the water come to just over top of my head, too black to see nothing through it. I shifts some looking for a smooth place on the bottom, but the pull of water knock me off my feets and carry me down. At first it feel like you been took for a ride but then I rolls over splashing back to where Buddy is.

"Thought I about lost you, Elijah," he say.

"No sir," I says. "You ain't."

I ask Momma if we could go back east but she say no Elijah you recall we don't got no house there now since that one catched fire and burned to the ground. So I don't talk no more about it. I stays inside all day when I don't go to school but it be like inside ain't no better than outside because if The Snatcher come for you, it don't make no difference where you hiding.

Momma get me and Buddy jobs at Mister Shelby's restaurant down by the train station, and I been saving my money. I got me a plan to take Momma and Buddy and go on back east to McDuffie County where we come from. Even if we ain't got no house there, I bet we could see where it was. They's lots in a house don't burn all the way to nothing.

We could go in a month if I don't spend none of my pay. We could take the Trailways out and then it'd be just me and Buddy and Momma living in a little place with a window in the kitchen like she want, a screen porch, and room so I could get me a bird. We'd keep all the doors wide open all day long and even at night in the summertime and won't have to worry about no strangers or nobody bothering us. I'd get me a blue parakeet, one of them birds that has a tiny sweet voice to sing and won't scare you with no talking and trying to sound like a person.

We could all of us get work in Warrington or Thomas and come home in the evening and set on the screen porch and be quiet. I'd find us a place where they ain't no dogs barking all the time and nobody coming into your yard who don't have no business with you. It'd be a long rise up to the front door so we could look out in every direction up the road and see what was coming.

Robbie Lynn

PEOPLE touch me all the time but I keep thinking it's never going to be them again, it's never going to be them, and then sometimes I close my eyes or turn my back and it is them, all their smells and looks and their voices saying they'd see us in the morning. At work somebody says give me your hands Roberta and she paints my fingernails and she holds one of her own hands under my jaw to pluck my eyebrows or draw lines where there aren't any and erase them where there are. In the mirror I look like my father done up and pretending to be my mother. It's funny and I stand there smiling at myself until dresser and makeup trade a look between them and hustle me on back into the studio. Even then I wave good-bye. I'm going a little crazy but I don't mind all that much.

The back of the photographer's hand comes up to my face like it's going to be a slap but then tenderly, tenderly, chin up, look to your left, lean this way sweetheart. We'll drive out to the polo grounds, or somebody's long driveway on Habersham Road. We'll go to Jonesboro down that same goddamn fucking highway and look for the exact spot where Tara stood, and I'll stand on it, a rocky field in the wind, or if there's no wind, then facing into a box fan that runs off the van's engine.

Mostly I'm shot with my eyes closed because that's what's in fashion, these models who look to be sleepwalking all dressed up. They have me in lipstick the color of a bruise. It makes my mouth look like it's been pressed against someone else's mouth for hours.

A hundred fifty proofs for the fall catalog came in last week, three days before they got killed. All black and whites, taken downtown. I spread them out on the kitchen table where they were repotting an azalea. I remember their hands black with potting soil and how they couldn't touch. I held the pictures up for them.

Gracious, Robbie, he'd said, you look bigger than the buildings, and later he cut out one of the proofs to sit on his desk at work. That's your Robbie Lynn? they said to him. Jesus, Sam, she's all grown up and she doesn't look a thing like you. But they're wrong, I look exactly like him. We both have dark hair and hard chins and in this picture he had on his desk, my hair is blacker than the wrought iron and the edge of my chin harder than all the steel and glass jutting into the sky behind me.

In the picture she liked best I'm sitting on a low stool beside an open window with my legs straight out, one knee coming through the folds of a white bathrobe. I'm staring out the window across 15th Street, seeing the south end of the High Museum. She said she liked it with my face turned half away, she said it was me that's all.

I remember driving down that same street with them when I was twelve, right before Sam was born, and waking up to look at that same window and seeing a man's body, naked and pearl white, angled toward me. Just then he arched his back and I felt a long ache start deep down in my belly. Hot light opened around my face and I turned my head away fast but not before the man saw and held up his hand. My mother was reading a map and my father had his eyes on the road. I was alone in the world with that man's body, its horrible lightness and darknesses already inside me. For a long time I was afraid he'd hunt me down and make me admit to what I knew. Now I feel different and when we walked into that house last month to do this shoot, I wanted him to be there, to touch my face and tell me how long he'd been waiting.

And then I'm at the top of the Peachtree Plaza, posed against a window in the cocktail lounge, the one that moves in its own orbit high over the city. You see me from the side, the clothes, the face, and then off to my left and stretching below, the whole of downtown spinning slowly away. I'm in a Glen plaid business suit and there's a black briefcase next to me on one of the glass tables. The eyes are open wide like I'm trying to take everything in. It's a face that says *There's no one coming. There's no one out there for me. There's no one out there.*

Oh I get it, Daddy said. You're a lawyer after a day at the office. I'd know that look anywhere, been grinding bones to butter your bread.

I think I'm supposed to be waiting for someone, I told him.

You look exhausted, my mother said, wiping her hands down the sides of her shorts and carrying the proof sheet over to the window. She stood there for a long time letting the picture work on her.

I wouldn't buy that suit, she said.

I know already this picture won't be in the catalog when it comes out at the end of August. Instead it will be Addie Ferguson in the same outfit sitting at one of the glass tables and laughing while a man tosses goldfish crackers into the air and catches them in his mouth. What you can't see is him throwing these little fish higher and higher, and her holding out her hands to catch them for herself, hoping the cocktail lounge will spin far enough and fast enough to bring them right to her.

You can't ever move far enough or fast enough to catch them.

I feel bad for Mr. Donnellan. He wanted to do a better job on them so there could be a viewing. We were in his velvet office where all the furniture has rounded corners, chairs, desk, couch, tables, sideboard stuffed with kleenex. There are times though, he said, the trauma comes in such a way, and then he stopped himself and asked if I'd like to sit down maybe have a sip of something. I said no in all honesty I had to do a luncheon show in the Magnolia Room at Rich's, ten different ensembles in white linen and try not to meet the eyes of my mother's friends who would all be there, eating their sandwiches with the damn crusts cut away and God I hope not weeping at the sight of me.

I'm bringing my brother in tonight, Mr. Donnellan.

You are, he said, turning to face me and then looking down at his folded hands. I wouldn't recommend it Miss Wilkins.

It'll be worse if he doesn't, I said.

He wants to see them one last time. You know, say goodbye. It's only fair. He holds his breath and turns blue and faints and it scares the shit out of me. If he doesn't he'll never get over it. These are all things I could say.

We'll be here at eight, I said.

Sam didn't cry and I didn't cry but Noreen did and Gus did. For a minute I hated seeing them that way. It made us strange with each other and I stopped knowing them a little bit. Ray wasn't there.

Afterwards I took Sam back to Grandma Wilkins's, put him to bed, and lay beside him for a long time. He wants to know how it happened. He asks over and over, but always one part of the story doesn't fit, the rain or the truck or the exact spot. Then he says *How do you know*, not mean but sleepy, like it was only part of a sentence, a question there's more to, only he's too tired to get all the words said out loud. It makes me go cold and I lie there a little while longer feeling my throat close up and seeing the streetlights swim in my eyes. I put my fist in my mouth, get up and go outside to stand by the garage, trying to be quiet. Each sound breaks from my lungs in the thin sharp cry of an animal being left behind and I listen to this noise like I'm not the one and it's coming to me from somewhere deep in the woods behind Grandma Wilkins's yard. Then it's Ray's voice whispering my name over and over, *Robbie*, sounding like all the other names lost children call out at night.

Gus

DEAR Billy, it's been three weeks and Noreen's daddy's still missing, but you know, you don't do anything different. You hate yourself for it but you mark off the days on your calendar, your fingers, or what have you. My arm's healing up fine and Grandma's teaching me all her card shuffling tricks in place of the doctor's exercises. Last night a girl we know who's older had a debutante party and ten of her guests caught on fire. The theme was Hawaiian Luau and some of the ones in authentic grass skirts were standing too close to the grill. Robbie says man-made fabrics go up like nobody's business. We heard the whole story from a model friend of hers whose eyebrows got singed. I told her she'd be a fool not to try for disability.

Robbie does better these days, her and Sam and her grandma don't always go around with that look like they've just been gut shot and haven't quite figured it out yet. Robbie's the big model in all the back-to-school catalogues, or she will be when they come out in August. Noreen and I get our old jobs waitressing at the Brookwood. This summer we're doing all the odd shifts, eight till after midnight and again first thing in the morning at 5:30. The round trip, we call it, mostly because with the train station next door, you get both sets of passengers from the Crescent, northbound at midnight and southbound at dawn. You remember how we always did like it that way, being never quite sure what day it is.

Ray's working there too, only it's just a few shifts so he can keep regular hours searching for his daddy. The three of us look out for each other, even though we don't say that's what we're doing. I'm fine and Noreen's mostly fine but Ray keeps breaking glasses. He says they just fall through his fingers and then to show how it happens he opens his hands wide, palms up like he's asking you for something.

He's going to quit the Brookwood altogether when his friend from Vermont gets here. Noreen called him up because she was worried about Ray with the driving around and the breaking glasses and all. Ray says his name is Joe Ithaca but that's not his real name. Anyways he's a Vietnam vet who lost one eye over there and now deals in antiques and curiosities, all of which makes him good at finding stuff you need.

As Ray tells it, they met in the public library in Burlington. Ray had hitchhiked the twelve miles from school on Saturday for some peace and quiet, and the library seemed like a good place to look for it. Instead he came across Joe Ithaca wandering through the shelves. Joe showed him how books on firearms and books on writing compositions shared a pair of bookends and Ray knew he'd found himself a bosom buddy.

For now, I'm glad he's where Noreen and I can keep an eye on him. There's a lot of that kind of watchfulness here this summer, two other boys we look after, brothers named Buddy and Elijah Johnson. Their mother cleans house for Mr. Shelby who just bought the Brookwood, and she asked him to hire them for the summer, to keep them out of trouble. Back in May, Elijah's best friend got lost on his way home from school and it turns out his body was the one we found in the river. Her boys were having nightmares, Mrs. Johnson said, they were curling up, especially Elijah. He wasn't running around like he used to. He wasn't spending his money, he was saving it. He wouldn't visit his friends. They were both mostly afraid. They were wondering what it's like to be lost forever.

Every day I imagine you walking in the front door the way you used to this time last summer. I never get much further than you come up behind me, put one hand on my shoulder, and say my name. I remember times when I was holding a tray or filling ketchup bottles or once it was handing a woman a steak knife I just about put through her heart. I can't remember what I said then, but I like to think I didn't start or cry out. Maybe I turned around calm as you please and asked how many's in the party just like it was anyone in off the street.

One evening I'm counting tips and slipping the bills into my wallet when I come upon that first picture of us I thought I lost and had such a fit about a year ago. Well, it takes my breath away coming out of the blue like that. I push my chair back from the table and wait for it to pass, that feeling of being pulled up by my hair, clean to the roots.

Alls I want to do is get rid of that picture as fast as I can. I take a package of matches from the bowl on top of the cigarette machine and carry them and the picture into the stockroom. I have to confess I set fire to it and I said Billy, go, please go. It takes a long time to burn, but I stand over the sink watching the edges curl up into a scroll as the paper bubbles and turns black. When it's done, the ash in the sink looks like a dead leaf that's crumbled and gray from being walked over. Buddy Johnson is standing behind me.

"I thought I smelled fire," he says.

He doesn't ask what I'm doing, he just looks over my shoulder into the sink and says he'd know fire a hundred miles away.

"My brother Elijah burnt a whole town once, and we ain't never told nobody. It was Boneville, Georgia, where we lived before we come on up to Atlanta. We was cooking us a lunch when Momma and Daddy was working and Elijah he took me out and left the stove on and when we come back, that house was gone and look like the whole street too. We told Momma we didn't know what happened."

"That's some story, Buddy," I say.

"It's true."

Buddy has a way of looking at you that makes it hard not to take him at his word, mostly though what does it is a scar on his right cheek, a pink spot the size of a quarter with lines running out from it in six directions. Noreen thinks he's marked by God, but the truth is, he was bitten by a dog there, and that's how it's healed. Still you come round to believing that Noreen's partly right and you stop what you're doing whenever Buddy starts to talk, just long enough to decide it's not the message you've been waiting for, and you go on back to work.

"Boneville?" I say.

"Yes ma'am. It's some maps you can still see it on, way over east of here, but it's mostly gone. Elijah say they keeps the name on the map cause they's stuff don't burn all the way, like our frigidaire, he says it's probably still standing there in the street. It's the heavy cold things don't burn nohow."

He looks down into the sink.

"Not like that," he says.

Elbert & Ross

WE told you so, we says.

We said they was sure to return to wait our tables this summer, them girls, the dark one and the light one who done got with Jesus, both standing there in the vestibule and beautiful fit to blind you. Then we turns to the boy they brung with them. We knows who he is by his looks.

"You must be the baby brother," we says. "We hear you a deep one. We hear you keep your own witness. Where you been all this time, son?"

"Vermont," he say. "In school."

"School," we says, turning away. "School." We ain't much on school.

We takes him back behind the register and the tables into the kitchen, where Elijah's doing dishes and we fixing to make a stew. We picks up a red onion and points the knife straight at that boy's chest.

"What you learned in that yankee school?"

"I don't know exactly," he say. "I'm not done yet."

"Not done yet!" we yells out. "Not done yet! Story of this life, not done yet. 'Hey y'all' one of them little gals be in here saying, 'Y'all got them burgers done yet?' 'Not done yet, sugar,' we say."

Them gals look at they hands because they knows it's the truth.

"You learn math-a-matics?"

"Some," he tell us.

"How about cooking?" we says, kinda sly. We know they probably don't teach none of that.

"No, no cooking."

"Reading then?" we says. "Our momma said if you can read you can cook. But it don't work the other way round."

"Lots of reading."

"What you been reading, son?"

"Stories, poetry."

"You like that stuff?"

"Ross and Elbert knows some stories," Elijah tell him. "They'll say some of theirs for you if you ask them enough."

"I don't know if I like it," he say, cutting his eyes at Elijah. "I don't think I get it half the time."

"Well you know it's only about two things all the time," we says. "It's only about dying and love. You must of been learning some about them, ain't you?"

That question fly out through the air and bash its way around the kitchen, striking the pots and pans on they hooks so the room sounds full of shivering and whispering voices.

"No," he say, "nothing."

We tells him that's just fine. We says it means he's still among the living.

He go to stand by the back door where the wall fan bring in the draft. Outside, it's commencing to rain. He turn to face into the air and close his eyes. All of a sudden, we know he's thinking about his daddy. We know because we thinking about ours too.

We gots more questions we could ask him because we just questioning kind of folks. What do love feel like, we could say, and he tell us he don't know, and we say it feel like burning up in your heart and leaving nothing behind. Next we like to ask then if that's love, why ain't the whole world dying from it, and if he don't know, we say well they is because you can't never get away from the light of such fire. It be like the sun and down here the days is long and the evenings stretch on like to be forever and you got to wait, moving your chair further away from the window so you don't get blinded or burnt by the way the sun go down in June.

64

This is all the poetry we knows. Poetry is everything in this world you don't understand till it come and knock you upside the head. Or you may prefer to think we just crazy.

Ray

I'M learning to make a bird out of an apple. Ross says for a bird it's all balance, thin edges of flesh cut and resting inside one another to make the wings. We do radish roses too, and he holds his hand over mine on the paring knife so I can get the feel of the cut. He and Elbert, they talk all day long in the kitchen like it's somebody just left the room, raising their voices to call after whoever it was and looking off past my face. At first I thought they were blind and when I saw them reach for those knives I was thinking I won't last an hour here, even if they do have that blind man's sense for whatever's between them and the vegetable of the day. But blind is about the last thing they are.

Elijah Johnson's not blind either, he watches everybody all the time and after an hour of watching me he says I remind him of the Wise Man. He says, you know the one I mean, Ray Gresham, calling me by my whole name, the Wise Man, the prophet of Trinity. I do know the one, the man who stands on the corner of Trinity Street and Peachtree watching traffic and sometimes asking people for quarters. He wanders around downtown at night and knows things nobody else knows.

"He's white too," Elijah says, "but don't nobody bother him. He can tell folks what's already on they minds."

Elbert and Ross listen and nod their heads.

"We know him from when we first come to Atlanta," they say. "He used to could talk more then. Once he was on the evening news. He used to tell stories and get folks to pay him."

"You tell us the story about the twenty-five children," Buddy Johnson says.

"We ain't got the patience for it now," Ross and Elbert say. "Anyway you boys done heard it enough to last a lifetime."

Later in private they tell me it's the story of a man who has twenty-five children and loses them all. He says Buddy and Elijah like it so much because it scares the bejesus out of them, but then when they stop and think, they remember it's just a story.

"But ain't nothing in this world just a story," they say, raising their black bony fingers to their lips.

At midnight, I count the day's tips, then tell Noreen and Gus not to wait for me. I leave by the back door and walk all the way downtown. A police car follows me for ten blocks between 16th and Harris until I start to duck into the hotels to ride the glass elevators and throw pennies thirty floors down into the fountains.

At the corner of Trinity, I nearly trip over the Wise Man sitting cross-legged in the doorway of Trinity Shoes, but then I can't think why I wanted to find him in the first place. He doesn't look all that wise, just crazy or drunk, pitched back against the glass door, under a smeared arc where his head's rolled from side to side. I stand in front of him for a few minutes and he just stares, closing one eye and trying to get a fix on me. All around us, the night cracks open in blasts of music from car radios and the regular sweep of headlights around the corner. Then it closes up again. That's the only way I can explain it, all of downtown like a door opening, then shutting before you can get a look inside. I start to ask him a question, maybe about his name or what he's doing here, but I don't know how the words are going to come out, so I keep quiet. I give the old man all the change in my pockets, all my first night's tips, and walk on home, taking the side streets that run along the expressway. I keep thinking how anything can happen to me now, and how I'm just waiting for it to.

I'm going to find you, even if it takes my whole life.

Elbert & Ross

WE tells the same one again and again like it be a lesson but it don't make no difference in this town.

There's a old nigger you see, once upon a time, and his wife, who has twenty-five children. They was all of them good and beautiful but times was bad, real bad and folks got to be fearing they own shadows. But folks is folks and they gots to eat so every morning when the peddler come past they house selling meat without no bones, they buys it. The old nigger keep asking why this meat don't have no bones and the peddler he say because bones is heavy and meat be cheaper without. When his wife fry up that meat she go to crying and when the old nigger ask her why she say she don't know except the smoke and the fire sting her eyes.

When a man gots twenty-five children he don't be thinking about all of them all the time and he can't always see if two or three is missing. He know the first and the last but thems in the middle gets jumbled up some. You ask any father if it don't be the truth. One day though he gather them all up and he count just fifteen. He counts again then, three and four time. Then he gets worried but he come to decide they must of been at they grandmomma's down the road. He's thinking on this and he go to stand at the door to his house, right in front of a big stone pushed half out the ground and blocking his view. He's thinking about his children and how he might like to go fetch them at they grandmomma's, and he hears voices singing high and lonesome like the choir do at benediction time. He raise

73

that big rock and he see a mess of bones and them bones start to singing louder. He put his hand to his mouth and fall to the ground because he know these bones is the bones of his children.

That old nigger's wife, she die of grief right there in the yard. The nigger took a long journey to find that peddler and when he do find him, he kill him with just one word. He say *you* and that's all. Then he come home to bury his children's bones in the cemetery and he live the rest of his days by hisself, praying for forgiveness.

After that they likes to hear the real story of our life, about Daufuskie Island where we was born, and the tarpaper house we grown up in. We tells them we may be brothers and we may be not. We tells them our grandmomma was clairvoyant and sometimes we sees with her eyes. We knows spirits and we hears they voices talking to each other. We say Elbert and Ross is only two of our names and the others is secrets we ain't never told nobody. We got sisters named July and August and we was in love with a gal called herself Thursday. We say after the boll weevil come and kill off the cotton and the white folks come and kill off the oysters we left them bloody marshes with a box of saltines between us, fell asleep for a heap of years, and woke up in the kitchen of the Atlanta Hilton with paring knives in our hands.

That morning, when we look down at ourself and seen the A-H for Atlanta Hilton acrost the bosom of them white shirts, we knew we done arrived. It told us *ah. Ah.* That's the sound you go to making when your body and your soul finds peace. That shirt was trying to give us a message. It was trying to tell us to stay right where we was. So we listened and we stayed. We gots some usefulness here. It ain't all been revealed to us yet, but we knows we got it, and it be coming soon because we getting on. Soon we be putting off this life and go walking back to the water. The water brung us in and the water set to take us away.

We gets usefulness from our grandaddy, who got him clair-voyance too, and he teach us his prayers and spells. He say the foxes of the forest got hole, the birds of the air has nest, but Master we poor son of man got nowhere to lay down weary head. He say when you hear the pig holler it fixing to rain. Pour kerosene round your house to keep off snakes and mix up ashes and chicken feathers to put the hex on somebody.

He died when we was boys, but we can see it like it was yes-terday, that old body weighted with stones and sent on down the Savannah River so his spirit could keep moving. In the morning, the young gals and the womens washed his sheets and cut them up to make clothes for the children, little white shifts and trousers.

Seems like we ain't never gonna take 'em off in this world.

Some of our usefulness is driving Buddy and Elijah home at night. Mr. Shelby he give us a car but all we go is down Peachtree and over to Atlanta Avenue. We keeps Grandaddy's old peacemaker loaded under the front seat and when we all get out to walk acrost the street to they momma's apartment, one of us tuck that gun into the waist of his trousers, and for those few minutes, them boys ain't afraid of nothing. We ain't never used no gun before cause we know it's the devil's right hand you be holding. But lots is changed and now could be we sing the devil his own song.

We got this idea about it all, the missing children and the murders. We been thinking about them children out there and these ones we got in here feeding folks. We can't say why, but we been visited by a notion that when we die, it'd all stop, all the snatching children and the killing. We can't say no more about it. It's just a feeling come on us lately.

75

Noreen

FOR *my days pass away like smoke and my bones burn like a furnace. My heart is smitten like grass and withered. I forget to eat my bread.*

Say this prayer every day for nine days, and you will find what has been lost.

Saint Anthony of Padua, return my daddy unto me. Saint Christopher, saint of travelers, carry these heavy children across the river.

Do not leave money as grace has no price. Do not ignore this.

Momma thinks this is all foolishness and she says she'll lock me in the house until I start eating again. I tell her I'll break the locks and Ray says Noreen there's nothing left of you, you might could just slip under the doors.

Shush Ray, Momma says, then Noreen honey I know how you feel.

No Momma, I say, you don't know.

Where is your Father? The Nazarene answered you know neither me nor my Father. If you knew me, you would know my Father also.

Robbie Lynn

"TELL me the story of it again," Sam says.

"It was raining. There was a truck going the other direction."

He wants to memorize the night they died, but I wish he'd stop asking.

"Tell me again."

"There was a truck. It was outside Jonesboro. It was raining."

"Who was in the truck?"

"A man. I don't know his name."

"Where is he now?"

"Sam, I'm sorry, I just don't know."

When I see him at the back door of the studio, squinting in where the lights are, I know who he is right away. There are tears in his eyes even before he starts talking. He says he'd driven in off I-75 on his way to Macon with a load of sofa beds from North Carolina. He wanted to see his sister in Jonesboro and he was lost. We face away from each other while he talks. I don't want to see him, but I want to know all of it, every last minute. He tells and tells and tells.

Ray

"I seen you downtown, Ray Gresham," Elijah Johnson says.

"What was I doing?" I say.

"You wasn't doing nothing. You was just standing there outside the Hyatt looking up the street and then the police come by and told you to move along."

"You find your daddy yet?" Buddy says, real soft and looking me right in the eye like he knows the words and what's behind the words.

I don't say yes and I don't say no either.

"Your hair was flapping in the wind is how I knowed it was you," Elijah says. "Like to glow in the dark."

When Joe gets here, I'll be able to cover more ground. He knows how to travel fast and far without studying maps more than once or getting lost. On Saturdays up north we used to drive all over Chittenden County at the speed of light with him telling me how maps are really miraculous signs from on high and only to be used on special occasions or in direst need. He'd talk at me that way, this crazy preaching, until we'd pull into a dealer's driveway and then once we'd get inside his voice would go prayerful or like he was talking to somebody on their death-bed. People'd load up our arms and we'd carry it all out to the car, mostly junk as far as I could tell, a lot of rusty eggbeaters, canning jars, ice skates, harnesses, wagon wheels. We'd drive it all back to Burlington with Joe hollering again how much he loved this stuff, and then we'd get to work.

He'd make lamps out of Mason jars, grease up the egg-beaters, and mend snowshoes, which people buy to hang on the wall in their dens. We'd wash lace collars in huge tin pails of soap and bleach and Joe'd do the ironing. He'd get ten of these collars from around Colchester and they'd be gone in a day, and then he'd sell the iron, one of those old-fashioned kind you warm up yourself in the fireplace. Ladies came back into the store wearing the collars they'd bought and Joe would say something about how the white brought the light into their faces. He'd fold his hands over his heart and tilt his head to bring them into focus. Then they'd leave, usually after buying some wooden spoon they must've had a hundred of, and Joe'd say to me, kind of embarrassed, shuck and jive Ray, shuck and jive.

That wasn't really him though, buttering up his customers so they'd spend the extra nickel. Every time he told one of those ladies she looked beautiful in a lace collar, he meant it. You could tell by the way his voice would get softer and he'd smile and never take his eyes off her. Seeing him this way always made me homesick. Alls I could think was how much he must love his mother.

His father he hasn't spoken to in years, since he told Joe to go on and get his head blown off in the most stupid useless war ever. His two other sons had already lit out for Toronto and were calling collect every week. No son of mine, he said, and Joe said all right, no son of yours and joined up with the army. I know he misses his daddy though, I know it. You can tell in the way he likes it when the store is full of men, mostly vets just come in to shoot the shit. There's veterans all over Burlington, Vermont and New Hampshire. When I asked why they came up here, one of them said it's to be near Canada, so next time we won't make the same mistake. He laughed then but nobody else did. Joe just turned back to a lady who was asking about her china pattern.

He stood there behind the counter looking at her out of his one good eye and saying he could get any item she wanted, for a price. He tells her he's best with odd pieces, the stuff you need one more of to complete the set. He calls them the dish-enfranchised and this time everybody in the store laughs.

One day though it was just the two of us, and he was trying to fix a demitasse but it was in about twenty pieces and after a while he starts shaking his head and all the color and joy runs out of his face.

"This happened to a guy standing right next to me," he said, pointing at the shards. He looked at me, then off over my shoulder. "I guess it's why I'm doing this hightailing all over creation for a lot of broken machinery. There comes a time when you figure you'll never outrun what's happened to you in this life, so you go back and immerse yourself. You get it out of your system by making it be your system. People mean a lot of different things when they say they're going to pick up the pieces."

If I were a girl, I would've walked over and put my arms around him, but I'm not so I just stood there kind of hoping he could read my mind and see what I intended.

The only antique in the store he won't ever sell is a book of poems by Robert Service. He picked it up at an estate sale in Bennington, meaning to unload it himself, but he started reading "The Shooting of Dan McGrew" and now he's never going to part with it.

"Don't you fucking love it when people's names are what they do? I mean a way of life, man, not a job. Names are sacred, Ray. Don't ever forget that. Here's a man whose goddamn name is service. Service. Listen to this:

> I've clinched and closed with the naked North,
> I've learned to defy and defend.
> Shoulder to shoulder we have fought it out,
> But the wild must win in the end.

I'm the wild, Man Ray," he says, reaching under the counter for his car keys, "and you're the wild too. Now let's go. We got some lovely old ladies to haggle with."

Back in March it was my birthday and he gave me a gun, a Harrington Richardson 20-gauge with an interchangeable rifle barrel. I'd shot guns before, at bottles and mirrors and busted lawn mowers, but never anything moving, and I never had one that was mine. I'm pretty handy with it now, but Joe had to show me where to stand, how to sight down the barrel, how to follow traps in the sky. He's taught me to shoot the way he does, like every time it's a new idea, something that just occurred to him. Between shots, he'll bring his 12-gauge down to his side, the barrel running parallel to his right leg. To start with the gun shouldered isn't right, he says. It's never going to be like that in life. You're never going to be that ready.

Then when the trap goes into the air, it's like Joe's whole body goes up with it. It hit me the first time I saw it, he looks like he wants to fly, but you don't ever think of Joe that way, dreamy and all and escaping from gravity, so I kind of laughed at myself. But I can't get it out of my head, this picture of him trying to break away from the earth.

For a long time I couldn't hit anything, then one day he told me to aim and he came around to stand in front of me, looking into the mouth of the gun.

"You're opening the wrong eye. Try the other one. That's it. Now draw a bead on me."

He stood there staring into the gun, making himself a target, much longer than he had to. All the time I was wondering if it was a mirror for him, his one black eye and the gun's each trying to stare the other down. I was thinking this and I still didn't shift my grip or swing the barrel over past his right or left shoulder.

Back then, I was already starting to like how a gun feels against your body, how it kicks into your shoulder the way one kid'll push another kid when he's trying to start a fight. I like the press of cold metal on my face, even the way it pops me on the cheekbone every time I fire. It feels like hearing a voice, strange as that sounds. *Sure, you pull the trigger,* it says, *but I'm doing the work.*

Now, back here at my mother's house, I take up the shotgun when nobody's home and aim out the window at birds and squirrels, but it isn't loaded. It'll take a while before I can shoot at a deer or any living creature. Animals seem human to me sometimes. Once I tried to explain this to Joe, but I don't think he got it.

I can see myself as an old man still trying to explain it. I'll be eating breakfast in one of those diners Joe likes to find off the beaten path and I'll clean my plate so there's nothing left to do but get up and leave. Then something crazy'll come over me, my eyes going out of focus and me standing up at the table in front of the sun so it seems like it's coming right out of my head.

And that's what they'll say, too, *out of his head*, but everybody in the place listens when I start to tell them how easy it is for a girl to turn into a deer and all the different ways it can happen. Sometimes you'll be with her and before your very eyes her eyes go dark and scared, her skin white and soft at the throat, and her legs put on flesh and long muscle. Or maybe you'll glance up at the sky for just a split second and look back to see her all deer, bounding away from you into the woods. Or the saddest is you leave her a girl, and she has to go away and can't come back. Then it's like you're dreaming and she'll come to you at night and show herself white and tan like she used to get in summer. She'll say this is what she is now and how their call was stronger than anybody's, even yours.

A few people'll get up and leave because they can't take it and they hate me for telling this story. They'll say you shouldn't talk about what's in your heart because now it's in theirs. The mothers will cry, especially the ones with young boys who could have this happen to them. Most just shake their heads because they really do know after all, a lot more than they ever dreamed.

At my mother's house, I sit in the window and aim and hear Joe's marching songs in my head.

> I gotta girl that lives on a hill,
> She won't do it but her sister will.
> I gotta girl in Lackawanna,
> She knows how but she don't wanna.

"About your control, Ray," Joe used to say, "make up your mind that you won't flinch."

I aim into the sky and pull the trigger, remembering how the gun cracks against my cheek and how I always looked down, thinking my face must have shattered and fallen to the ground in pieces, but it was never there.

Gus

DEAR Billy, can you tell me where exactly you are right now? On the nights we all work the late shift, I drive, and when my last tables are cleared and set up again for breakfast, I wait outside on the back steps, facing away from the kitchen toward the railroad tracks. A long arm of light falls out of the open door, over my head and down the steps into the parking lot. It's cooler out here facing south into the sleeping neighborhood behind Brookwood Station. Darkness always feels that way, you know, cold at the heart. Shadows move in and out of the light behind me, and I hear Ross and Elbert talking to Noreen and to each other in single words between the rattling of waxed paper and tinfoil. They're talking about pies, what kind each of them likes best and why it is that no one ever asks for the lemon meringue.

The midnight train slips into the station. It's always a surprise to me the way it arrives dark at first then gaining light from the passenger windows and I've always thought you could taste it in the food here, that iron and bitter oil and electricity, but nobody ever complains. They say bring it on sweetheart, more, more, faster, faster. They've been saying it all day.

Tonight Elbert calls outside asking if I've seen Buddy and Ray come in from the dumpster. I tell him I haven't and he says oh Lord. Elijah turns off the dish sprayer and comes to stand in the doorway alongside Elbert. He's big for fifteen, bigger than Elbert and Ross put together, but the size of him makes you relax a little. If there was trouble, he'd know what to do.

"Them boys," Elbert says. "I should never let them out of my sight." He turns and reaches his hand out to touch Elijah's shoulder. "When you seen them last?"

"A half hour ago."

Elbert puts his cleaver down on the shelf beside the door, then picks it up again.

"Maybe they're out front," I say. "I'll go look."

"No, honey," Ross says, "I'll go. You stay here and wait with Elijah."

There in the doorway the air vibrates on my bare arms and legs, raising the skin in goosebumps. A breeze rustles around in the high branches of the pine trees behind Brookwood Station.

The Brookwood shares a dumpster with the train station and with whatever comes from the on-ramp to I-75 south where it passes in front of a knee-high stone wall. They never have had a dumpster here because Shelby won't pay for it. He's a generous man in most ways, but Elbert says Shelby doesn't think trash is trash unless you have to haul it some distance.

Noreen comes out from setting her tables.

"No sign?" she says. "Where is that dumpster anyway?"

"No," I say, turning around to look up at her. "No sign. I was just thinking Shelby needs to get with the modern way of doing things."

"Hey," she says once, then again louder, stepping over me and down the steps. There's somebody walking out of the shadows at the far end of the parking lot. When he gets closer to the light, I can tell it's Buddy, and when he sees us, he stops walking and waits for Noreen and me to get to where he is. He's holding one hand over his face and there's blood pouring out of his nose, coming through his fingers and running down the front of his shirt.

"Elbert," I yell without looking back. "Ross."

We get Buddy into the kitchen and clean up some of the blood with dish towels and aprons.

"Shit, Buddy, who you run into out there?" Elijah says.

Buddy just shakes his head.

"It's broke," Ross says, moving his fingers tenderly over Buddy's face. "Now you didn't do this just by falling down, did you?"

Buddy still won't say anything. He keeps on crying, the tears coming in a silent wash, mixing with blood and running into the corners of his mouth faster than we can wipe it away. Elijah stands beside him holding a blue dish towel, carefully, like it's the one thing in all the world that has to be kept clean.

"What happened to you?" he keeps saying.

"Ray," Buddy finally says. "I must of made him mad."

He curls his hands into fists and brings the right one up to his own face, looking surprised all over again.

"*Ray?*" Elijah's eyes go wide. "What'd you say to him?"

"It's something about his daddy gets him furious."

There's a shuffling on the steps outside and we all turn around to see Ray standing in the doorway looking back at us. His face is closed up, not giving anything away. Elijah drops the blue dish towel and moves toward the door, but Ross catches him up by the back of his tee shirt.

"Easy," Ross says, "easy now." His voice gets quieter and quieter until it's just sounds.

Elijah's the one who calls the police, but nobody finds out until later, long after Elbert has left to take Buddy up to the emergency room at Piedmont and we've all gone home. When Noreen tells me the next morning Ray's been arrested, I don't think about Elijah, and I still don't think about him a day later when all the charges get dropped and Ray comes home.

I don't think about Elijah until the first time he jumps Ray in the parking lot behind the Brookwood, blackens his eyes, and breaks his collar bone. By then Elijah's quit working for Shelby. Buddy says he's washing dishes and sweeping floors somewhere else, but he won't say where.

"Elijah don't come home no more," Buddy tells us. "He been gone three days, then he come back and Momma she carry on and raise her hand to him and he say right quick *Momma, I got work.* She put her hand away and go to hug him but he get like a stone then he was out the door."

He's not gone though, he's everywhere. At least that's what Ray says. He says you'd recognize the cut of Elijah's huge shoulders and his profile when it's framed in the streetlights glowing along Peachtree.

When Mrs. Johnson comes in to ask if we've seen Buddy, we all feel sick. She runs her palm along the back of a chair while she talks and I look at her hand move because I can't look at her face. The smell of cooked food hangs gray in the air and when she's finished asking, alls there is to listen to is the sound of the grill hissing out in the kitchen.

Two investigators come looking for Ray. I'm leaning against the front register when they pull up in a dark blue car. Everything about them is dark, suits, ties, their same mustaches growing the exact same way.

"Hey," I say to Noreen, "either it's a church group or it's trouble."

"What do you know about church groups, Gus?" Noreen says.

"Either one, it be trouble," Elbert says.

They come inside and have to stand in the doorway because I'm blocking the aisle past the candy case.

"You got a Ray Gresham works here?" the one closest to me says.

"What if we do?" I say.

"It ain't good for business to act that way," the taller of them says in a low voice.

"Ray," I call without turning my head or taking my eyes off the two of them. "Ray, you got company."

Ray comes out of the kitchen and all three of them go to sit at one of the back tables. I come over with the coffeepot, but the tall one waves me off so I set the pot back on its burner and take a long time cleaning tables to hear what they're saying. They ask Ray a few questions about where he's been lately and when he says right here, they ask if there's anybody can vouch for that. He makes a sweep with his good arm that takes in the whole of the Brookwood and all of us.

"You look a little tore up, son," the tall one says to Ray.

He tells them about Elijah Johnson, and they watch his hands move over the silverware.

"You ain't interested in pressing charges?"

"No," Ray says. "I'm not interested."

They tell Ray to stay where he can be found if need be, then they get up from the table, wishing us all a pleasant evening and smiling extra hard at me. This whole visit, it's just for show, I know it. Ray's not the one they want. Nobody wants these murders to be the work of a white boy. If it was, this whole town would burst into flames all over again.

99

Elijah

WE was playing and I was s'posed to be looking after him but I turned around to answer somebody calling my name and that's when it happen, that big old watch dog the Jacksons got done broke his chain and jump the fence and go to working on Buddy like it was his supper. Buddy ain't but six years old then and that dog was more than one hundred pounds. One hundred fifteen, I heard Mister Jackson bragging about the day before. It knock him down pretty hard and at first I hear Buddy laughing thinking that dog just going to lick his face, but then he start to screaming and his screams get to where they be like knives coming out his mouth and going into the air. Sometimes I can still hear them and even now any time I hear a child scream, I like to fall down and die.

Then they was two voices carrying on that way and when I could listen with my mind I hear that one of them voices is mine. That dog is still tearing into Buddy's face and I'm holding my own hand to my own face and when they lifts that dog away, its mouth was dripping with blood and I was still holding my hand to my face until Mister Jackson he say what's wrong with you boy, you ain't hurt but your brother is near tore in two and you ain't never said a word.

They carried Buddy past me and his eyes was closed and they was blood everywhere round a hole in his face. Folks kept asking *why didn't you say nothing, why didn't you say nothing* and I told them I was watching him real good and they say *real good ain't good enough.*

103

The first night Buddy stayed over in the hospital Momma she stayed with him and Daddy took me home. I made myself keep awake till Daddy done dropped off to sleep, then I ran out the house, acrost the back yard down crawling on my belly past Daddy's window. I worked myself down to the Jackson's carport where they is a pile of boards and I pulled loose one of the boards and crawled on back up to where that dog is sleeping over on his side of the fence. He waking up some now, but not fast enough so I cracks him hard over the head with that board. He stay where he is so I gets him another good one. Then he go to howling, just standing still with his new chain caught up in his legs. I hits him over and over until Mister Jackson, he come out and snatch that board from my hand and Miz Jackson, she take me up in her arms and she go to telling Mister Jackson I don't mean no harm. Then I like to hit her too for saying them words. I means harm. Ain't no cause to hit no dog with a board if you don't mean no harm by it.

Buddy has to stay in the hospital for a week. At first he got bandages on his face, then they strip them off and put in a tube so his face could drain out. All day long something like honey come from that wound and slide down that tube so you could see it drop into a bottle he have strapped to him. I still can't make myself say nothing to him, just stand by his bed watching that bottle fill up and get changed and fill up some more.

Momma get to acting funny then about Buddy and his face. She say to the nurses don't let him see what he look like, don't give him no mirror if he ask for one. You can see plain they thinks Momma's crazy, but ain't nothing they can do about it. Buddy be asking to see hisself, but they say not today sugar, maybe tomorrow you can see.

I stay there with him most every day after Momma go to work. We plays with the toys or watches TV but every day Buddy ask me what do he look like and he want to know more and more. I gets to thinking how I can't save him from seeing hisself just like I can't save him from that one hundred fifteen pound dog, but if I show him what he look like somehow it would negative that dog bite. This suffering it's a kind I could make to be over quick, and if any of it's my fault it going to be all my fault.

In the playroom downstairs from Buddy's room they's a big glass bowl of goldfishes. It look like a hundred fishes because they's a mirror back of the glass bowl. I take Buddy in there and I say to him look Buddy, look at the fishes real good. You see anything unusual about these fishes?

And Buddy, he just bend down and look and I see his right hand come up to his face real slow and he touch hisself around the tube while he watch hisself in the mirror, and then he say no Elijah, don't seem like nothing funny about them fish.

The doctor say he going to grow into his scar and he do. Now it ain't but quarter size with them lines going out from it like a star. He don't look like nothing else in this world and it ain't a day in my life I don't think about how he got that way. I made him go look at hisself because he need to know the truth about me. He need to know I could fail him that bad.

When I seen Ray Gresham walking by hisself at night, I gets a pain in my chest running clear between hate and love and I holds my hand over my heart to keep it from busting open. His legs is still bad where I knocked him down and he move real slow and have to stop every ten minutes to take him a rest. He making his way along Peachtree, going home I guess, letting the buses pass him by, so it look like he mean to walk the whole way. Once he stop to pick up a tree branch and strip off the twigs to make him a walking stick. It help him some to move faster, but it ain't much.

Right then it come on me, you are alone in this world and it ain't never going to be any other way. I get to thinking about Buddy and I like to cross the street and break Ray Gresham's ribs but I feel so weak and sorry I stay on my side and I fall to whistling, just so he know that empty space is lying there between me and him, dark and just a-waiting for its hour to come.

105

Elbert & Ross

IT be just they pictures, the names and no words in a line on the wall behind the register. Only they faces staring at folks while they pays for what they has to eat. Most folks looks once and say is that the missing children and we says yes and we leans in close to them and we ask if they's seen any of these faces.

"Look real good," we says.

"Oh no," folks says. "I'm from out of town. I don't know nothing about it. I come from Baltimore."

"You here now, ain't you?" we says.

Noreen

"YOU want to split Elijah's hours, Noreen?" Gus says. "Shelby says we can have them if we want. If you don't mind dish washing."

I don't mind at all and I imagine washing dishes might be just the right thing, the way my hands and arms are so cold all the time lately. I tell Gus I'll do all the washing and run the counter too, and she's happy to still be able to drift through the big dining room where she can see everybody coming in and going out and have them see her too.

Most of the people who eat at the Brookwood are strangers headed out of town on a train and while I'm feeding them I always think about who they might be, what least of whose brethren. Their bills don't usually add up to much because most of them eat alone. If there's two, a lot of times it means one's leaving and one's staying, and saying good-bye has never been known to make anybody real hungry. The customers I wait on all seem like they're trying to remember something important, staring out over their plates into the middle of the dining room. The men who come in alone will take off their wristwatches and set them down across the table to look at like it was somebody else there. If a lady is by herself, she'll drink her beer out of the bottle. She'll sit low in her chair and sigh, and she'll clean her plate.

Up until tonight I haven't had to wait on anybody I know, besides family and Robbie Lynn, but now I'm working the late shift and Mrs. Johnson comes in an hour too early for boarding on the midnight train north to Clemson. I know she's going to Clemson because she leaves her ticket on the table and has to come back for it.

She sits down at a table near the front door and orders without looking at the menu or me or anything else. Even in this heat she wants baked ham, mashed potatoes and red eye gravy with two ginger ales, and she finishes all of it, asking for more bread to mop up the gravy.

The food seems to bring her back into this world. She sits forward in her chair, rests her elbows on the table, and watches me clear away the plates then come back across the room. When I'm nearly in front of her, she looks away, and I see it happen, the very moment she fixes her eyes on the picture of Buddy we've got hanging up behind the cash register. Her eyes lock onto his and go wide and her head snaps back just a hair, not so anyone would notice if they hadn't already been watching her. Her eyes move up the whole row of pictures then down to Buddy, swinging back and forth in their sockets. The rest of her stays perfectly still.

"Mrs. Johnson?" I take care to keep my voice low.

"Yes?"

The way her shoulders drop makes me think it's a deep relief to her to be known.

"We're all keeping him in our prayers, Mrs. Johnson."

She nods and looks straight up at me. She doesn't say thank you, and if you stop to think about it, there's no cause for her to anyways.

When she comes back for the train ticket, I meet her at the door and wish her a safe trip.

"Same to you," she says.

I like this job the way I always have. Some days I think about spending the rest of my life giving strangers full plates of food and then taking away whatever they leave. Doing this, you don't think so much about your own hunger, blessed as it may be. You turn elsewhere, just like you're supposed to, and look after the strangers who come to you like the strangers always do in the Bible, searching for somewhere to bury their dead.

Joe Ithaca

I left Burlington first thing in the morning, heading south on Route 7, Georgia-bound. I pictured myself fresh out cutting a swath of daylight the length of the eastern United States, until I got to below the Mason-Dixon line and night would start to come on again. I wanted to say it out loud to somebody, yell at all the sleepers in their beds, wake up you sons a bitches, Middlebury and Brandon and Rutland where I pulled into a diner for breakfast.

By the time I hit north Bennington, the world was greener than I'd ever seen it, almost tropical, big trees tangled together, high, flat-faced hills, landscape that seemed to me this time through would admit no man entrance. It spooked me, if I own up to it. I pulled off the road in Hoosick, New York to call my mother in Richmond.

It was my Dad that answered the phone, so I hung up, thinking to try again later. I drove on 7, west toward Troy, but it was only a half-hour further, just outside Pittstown, that I stopped to call her again. These woods were getting to me something awful, the morning fog making the pine trees look like brown signposts with the sign part lopped off. If I'd stopped the car, gotten out and turned around once, I'd have been lost. The very road felt like it was sinking under my tires. I didn't see how I was going to get around Tomhannock Reservoir without sliding in off the shoulder. Somehow I got this notion that talking to her would make it all make sense. It was one of those ideas gets into your head and you can't explain it, except that you know it's right.

On the second try, here outside Ursula's Ursa Major Souvenirs, I get her on the phone.

"Did you just call?" she says.

"Yeah." She won't need an explanation.

"I thought so. Where are you? I hear trucks."

I tell her. I tell her I'm taking a vacation and I'm on my way down to Atlanta to help a kid find his father.

She doesn't ask a lot of questions, my mother. She figures I'll make my intentions clear to her in my own good time. I know it breaks her heart that the old man and I don't speak. She keeps at us both in her quiet way, telling me he's getting old and forgetful, covering the receiver and telling him *Joe's on the phone*, loud because he's also just about stone deaf. I'll hear some noises that sound like a helicopter far off and know that it's him talking, telling her he has nothing to say, the little blade of his voice chopping at the air around my head. I don't let it get to me anymore. I know how to settle my thoughts on the next piece of news I've got for my mother, the words I'll say as soon as she comes back on the line.

Today she tells me *Your father says you be careful down there. He says in Atlanta people'd just as soon kill you as look at you.*

I want to tell her he didn't say any such thing and she knows it. But then I'm not sure. I hang up the phone and think on it all the way through Troy and onto I-88.

I'm feeling more like myself now, but it's one long lonesome stretch of road to Binghamton. You drive toward Cooperstown and try to remember any single paragraph of James Fenimore Cooper to get you through, but all I can get are the two sisters out of *The Last of the Mohicans*, Cora and Alice, one dark-haired and one blonde, who always reminded me of the Parker girls from Richmond High School, one of them real prissy and the other probably out looking for some hot-blooded young brave at this very moment.

My thoughts go on like this, then there's a second or two when I'd think about that sentence my dad might or might not have said, and my heart seizes up for nearly a mile. I wait for it to pass, trying to gauge the grade of this land, keeping lookout for runaway truck ramps, even though I'm safe as sin in a Chevy Malibu. Seems like the highway from Oneonta to Binghamton runs all downhill, from the top of the earth to down in it, deeper and deeper where you cross the state line at Great Bend, Pennsylvania. You start to want to take your foot off the gas, open all the windows, and let fly. You want to take some chances. But here I am, sliding down the ankles of the Adirondacks, going slower and slower trying to remember what my father's voice sounds like and how it might have said those words about just as soon kill you as look at you. Toward Ninevah, New York I can hear the soft drawl, the flat vowels, the higher register that his voice used to skip into when he'd run out of breath at the ends of sentences. Then it's my voice too, banging itself around inside this old machine. I hit the gas, pressing the pedal to the floor. I want to get there, get to Ray, his mother, his sister. I'm tired of being alone.

I make ace time between home and Binghamton, so I stop here for lunch. There's a Holiday Inn you can see practically from the New York State Thruway, a big new one, the kind of place there'd be a restaurant. They'd know how to get you lunch and let you get back on the road. This is fancier than most, eight stories of motel stacked on top of a glassed-in pool and a lobby that goes on for miles. The restaurant is supposed to feel like outside in the Orient, with red paper umbrellas and chopstick bird cages, so I sit myself down at a table with a good view of the gift shop and as close to the door as I can get. Being outside in an unknown Asian country wouldn't be my idea of a good time.

Next to the maître d's station, a girl is waiting for take-out. She orders a turkey club and two beers, and they bring her the beers first but forget to open them. I can see she has a real thirst on, so I stand up and reach across the table to hand her my

119

pocketknife. I don't even say "here," and she doesn't thank me, just opens the beers and hands back the knife. Her smile takes my breath away a little. It makes me want to do something else just to see it come across her face like that again. She lifts one of the beers by the neck and takes a long drink, breathing hard after the bottle leaves her lips. Her shoulders drop and when she turns and bends to set the beer back down on the table beside her, a hank of black hair falls across her face. At this moment, I wonder if I've ever seen anything like this woman growing all loose and sleepy before my very eyes.

She yawns then and I think how much I'd like to stop here and go upstairs and watch her eat and fall asleep with the television going on low and the afternoon coming on into evening and me not knowing a thing about her. Maybe I wouldn't even touch her, or just hold her hand until I was sure she didn't need me anymore.

The waiter brings her sandwich in its white styrofoam hamper, which she tucks under her arm. When he asks what room number to put on the bill, she tells him, and I say that number over to myself all through lunch, in fact all afternoon, dropping down I-81 into Pennsylvania.

Driving south, I imagine her upstairs in that room, eating her lunch, drowsing between the last bites and the second bottle of beer. I see her watching Phil Donahue, something she would never dream of doing in her life off the highway. It's a show about Vietnam vets, and I'm one of Phil's guests. I'm only doing it for the money because times are a little hard lately. I vow to myself in the network limo on my way to the studio that I won't say a word, and I won't commiserate. I won't let my voice get thick and halting on national television, won't give those whores the half hour of gripping human drama they want.

She's watching me, this dark-haired woman in a motel room in New York State, and she's falling in love with me right then and there. She's eating her sandwich more and more slowly, then finally she pushes the whole container away and comes to sit on the end of the bed, up real close to the TV. She watches me shake my head and keep silent when Phil asks about the innocent women and children at My Lai. Tears come into her eyes but she doesn't know why. She leans closer to the set so she won't miss a single word if I speak, but I never do. Her blood runs faster and warmer through the vast dark mileage of her veins when I look straight into the cameras. I am the man she's been waiting for all these years.

When Phil breaks for station identification, she gets up from the bed and goes to the window. She holds the beer bottle to her forehead and thinks how glad she is that it's raining because that's how her life feels to her these days. She looks across the parking lot and back down I-81 behind her, letting her eyes drift west toward Chicago, toward the set of Donahue's show, thinking how she'll go there tomorrow instead of north to Albany, Troy, Saratoga Springs, Glens Falls. She'll go to Chicago and find me in the lobby of my hotel or coming up the beach with all of Lake Michigan spread out behind me. There's nothing else she can do.

In every state, I stop at the Welcome Center for coffee and brochures, flirt a little with the nice ladies from the Chamber of Commerce, and leave with directions to the best antiques in four or five counties. They're always surprised to find a man in the trade. Sometimes I tell them I have a pretty good eye for the stuff and then they look at me hard for a minute, trying to decide if I mean it as a joke. Usually I have to laugh first and then they will.

When I get to Atlanta, I'll read all these brochures, the literature, as they call it. Most of what I pick up is battlefields, Gettysburg, Antietam, Bunker Hill, Harper's Ferry, Manassas, Fredericksburg and Spottsylvania, Cowpens, Chickamauga. I figure I'll play tourist on my way back north. Some of them were hard to pass by though, the battlefields close to the highway. You could see them coming at you from miles back, the ground hollowing itself out or rising up suddenly to form strongholds like Bunker Hill and Little Roundtop. Maybe it's just me, but I swear you can smell a battlefield on the horizon. The air would get full of a thin clean sweet smell, like before a rainstorm only with more bite to it. A guy I used to know said it had to do with decaying bodies, blood-soaked soil, and carbon half-lives. Whatever it is, he's part of it now, back at Kae San.

The only one I might have stopped at was Gettysburg. There's a story about my father's grandfather, a tinker from Philadelphia who spent the years before the war mending knives, splinting the broken legs of household pets, shoveling shit, and predicting the weather. He fought with Union troops at Gettysburg, and one morning when he was heeding the call of nature he was surprised by an infantryman from Georgia, who offered him tobacco, which he took, wished him long life, or at least the full light of another day, and then disappeared into the mist. It's the kind of story you'd never even consider doubting.

I like to picture my great-grandfather lying awake in the patch of wet grass he'd dropped into, thinking of the soldier from Georgia and not having a goddamn clue about what either one of them was doing still alive in that field. I can see him deciding he'd go to Georgia, as soon as the war was over. He was a smart man, and as such, he could predict more than the weather. He knew at Gettysburg which way that ill wind was blowing and he thought he might be useful down south, a man whose life had been spared by a southerner.

He never got to Georgia but he got through the rest of that dark morning in late June 1863, lying awake, squinting through the haze of stale powder and stinking humid air. I know he tried his damndest to listen too, through the groans and cries and whispers of the dying, trying to listen for the breathing of the man next to him whose eyes had stayed open all night. I know he wondered if those eyes could still see anything, and he thought of all the people he'd be willing to die for and prayed the only prayer he knew which was a lot of questions one right after the other.

He prayed he was close to God, prayed for a little bit of light, not daylight though. Maybe just a flame or lightning, enough to see a face, a jacket, the white of an eye.

And then just before he fell asleep, he asked God to let him die gloriously, but not today.

I know because it's every soldier's prayer, and it'll come back at the strangest times, like just before dawn, heading into Atlanta, Georgia, riding alone into a strange, murderous town with only your father's voice to guide you.

Robbie Lynn

KIDS had started getting finger-printed, that's how bad it was with the kid-nappings and the murders. I went to the post office with my parents and Sam to get his done. It was the last place the four of us went together. They drove down to Jonesboro that night to see my mother's mother and it was rainy and a goddamn semi hit them head on. Skidded out of his lane. He said he didn't even see them. I already know this, and I've known it for a month now, I'm just repeating it to make it come clearer or else go away.

I remember half thinking it was one of those June days that lets you know the kind of summer you're in for, air so full and hu-mid it's nearly crying all over you. Made me want to cry too, just to feel something really wet, instead of all that shadowy damp. We drove to the post office in Buckhead, all of us real quiet. That scared Sam even more and I was thinking I should tell him a story, make up something about his fingerprints, black magic going into the ends of his fingers, but the words wouldn't come, so I didn't say anything.

Inside was like the first day of school, kids running around everywhere hollering or crying, their parents trying to get them to be still. Tables were set up along the front windows and four women with ledger books and stamp pads sat behind them in folding chairs. Two were white and two were black, but they all looked like somebody's mother, and I couldn't help wondering where their own children were.

As soon as we walked in the door, Sam got into this trance. I'd seen him do it before, stand stock still in the middle of a room and watch the other kids, kind of reading their minds.

Mother said all children do it, searching for familiar faces, but the way Sam looks, his eyes gone wide and his hands clasped behind him, you think he might rise right up off the floor. He's convinced he's been in this world before, living another life. He says he and Bob Neal the weatherman were buddies at Normandy. Sam thinks Bob Neal got killed but he doesn't know for sure since they never found his body.

We get in line in front of one of the tables. Up ahead, the women are asking name height weight date of birth. Sam listens and then his lips start to move, practicing the answers so he'll be ready.

That's when it came on me, the closest thing I've ever had to a vision in my life, the air gathered up, coalesced over Mother's and Daddy's heads, thick and white like milk. It made doves or snowy egrets, and at first I thought I was fainting. I could understand where Noreen gets some of her ideas because I expected to see Jesus walk forth from behind the mail counter or come snapping out of the stamp machine in a long sheet. Then things were all clear again, the air smelled exactly like Clorox, and somebody behind us said it was going to rain.

I saw Sam's body quaver all over when the kid in front of him laid her hands on the ink pad, then it was his turn. My mother started to answer the questions, but Sam shushed her and gave the answers himself. He didn't know how tall he was, but he knew all the rest. Then when the woman reached across the table and said *Now honey, give me your hands*, Sam pulled way back and said no, he wasn't going to let her turn him into a black boy. Clear as a bell. All the women stopped themselves and looked at him. It came out later that's what he thought it was all about, white kids being somehow turned into black kids, starting with the tips of their fingers and spreading inward and upward, little white kids signing up to replace the black kids who were missing.

That was one of the last times I saw Sam in daylight. I know people can't really disappear, but that's what always happens isn't it, gone overnight? Now I know where he is, but they still won't let me see him much. He's been staying with Mrs. Whitaker, his kindergarten teacher, after she and some other people from his school decided an old deaf woman and an eighteen-year-old girl weren't right to take care of him. They came and got him in the middle of the night. I heard him cry out in his sleep and then nothing, maybe a car door slamming now that I think about it, but maybe not. They took him at night because they knew how it would be with me. They knew I'd tear them limb from limb and see the streets run with their blood before I'd let him go.

Without Sam there's nobody left, no way to remember Mother and Daddy. We could see them when we looked in the mirror in my grandmother's bathroom, standing side by side, Sam up on the rim of the tub.

"You look like her," I say.

"You look like him," Sam says. "Grandma calls it favor. She says you favor your momma."

We say their names over to ourselves until they're just sounds on their way back to oblivion.

I've already broken Sam out twice. Both times it was at night, and he slid out the window like letters through your front door, mailing himself into my arms. He was scared, sneaking along the back hedges and trying to look motionless, but I wasn't. This is my element, to be moving and still at the same time. You can see it in my portfolio. It's what I do for my living. We cut deep into the woods behind the house, farther and farther in until there's no light, no one to hear us. Sam starts to whisper to me then, talking about school, how it takes him so long to do his work at Mrs. Whitaker's because she asks him questions all the time. He thinks he may be in first grade for the rest of his life.

"When are you coming to get me forever?" he says.

"Soon, Sammy," I tell him.

We keep walking, heading now through the back lots to Noreen's house, where she and Gus and Ray will be waiting to swim. They will have cookies for us, soft ones that fall apart in your mouth, and ice cream not in her mother's blue china bowls but in paper cups. Sometimes it's tiny hamburgers from the Krystal, food that will make no noise. Sam and I are always hungry. It's how we miss Mother and Daddy, through these holes in our bellies that can't be filled up.

"Tell me the story of it again," Sam says.

"It was raining. There was a truck going the other direction."

He's still trying to memorize the night they died. He wants to get it straight.

"Tell me again."

"There was a truck. It was outside Jonesboro. It was raining."

"When are you going to come get me forever."

"Soon, Sammy."

When Ray's friend Joe gets to town, we'll go rescue Sam. I don't know how, but after that I'm thinking of going to live in Texas or leading mule treks down the Grand Canyon. It seems like no one could find you there. It's farther away than God.

In the morning, the photographer hisses at me, writhing behind his camera. *Your eyes, your eyes. What do you think this is? Raccoons for National Geographic? You're losing it, Roberta.*

Roberta is my stage name. Only policemen, photographers, and priests are allowed to call me that.

He takes children and young adults. He's very good with kids and he's working on a book of their pictures, but he's had to quit driving around the city looking for candids because the police kept stopping him. Once he was arrested for possession of a camera and other articles used to lure children. He told us he didn't mind at all, in fact, he was glad the cops were paying so much attention.

There's a picture in his studio of a black boy, about twelve. He's wearing dungarees and tennis shoes. His shirt's off, crumpled in one hand, and he's got his other hand on the back of his hip, pushing his belly forward. He's cutting his eyes at the camera like he knows a real good joke, but he's not sure you'd appreciate it enough, so he's going to wait and see. There's a length of black ribbon running around four sides of the picture, tied in a bow at the bottom.

"Look at that skinny little body," the photographer says. "How could you beat up that little body, then stick a knife in it seven times. Tell me, how?"

I know he's gone back behind his camera to cry. He's seeing me now, in this wool dress, blurry and unraveling. Someone must know how these things can happen. A truck? A rainy night on the road back from Jonesboro? A little boy like Sam?

If I twirl fast enough in this dress, the skirt will stand straight out. Underneath it, I could hide a hundred children. They would twine themselves around my legs. They would be warm. They would try to get back into my womb.

Ray's friend Joe will be here soon. He will know what to do. Ray says so and I believe him. Ray talks to me about where his father and Buddy Johnson might be and about Joe Ithaca.

"People don't just disappear," he says to me.

"Ah," I say but I know that already. Small animals disappear and bugs that fly into lightbulbs, fish turned sideways in the water, snow and other kinds of weather, but not people.

We're parked down the street from my grandmother's house. I'm touching his face, the raw swelling from his forehead to below the cheekbone. Elijah Johnson did this to him too, along with the collarbone. Elijah says the score still isn't settled. Ray shakes his head carefully. The score can never be settled, he whispers, he's fighting for Buddy now.

"Your hands feel so cool," he says. "Touch me here. And here."

The side of his face is open and moist. In a story I've heard, a girl falls in love with a man who runs a slaughterhouse. She comes to know him in the dark by the smell of blood that drifts out of his body. This is how I know Ray now. I want to bleed like he does, not secretly and slowly the way girls do, but everywhere and out in the open. His touch can do this for me, here in the dark, make the wounds rise to the surface of my skin from way down below. He can do so much for me. Everywhere his hands move, the blood rises and gathers just under the surface of my skin, a line of electric bruises running between my breasts where he's pushed open my shirt, welling up between my legs, where his hand is now opening a bruised flower, carefully, unfolding, fluttering there, a bird beating its wings, then battering them against the air. All soft wet air I rise up to take him in, rising and falling, the two of us bruising ourselves against each other until blue contusions cover our bodies, the blood about to break through the surface of our skin.

"Am I hurting you?" he says.

"No," I tell him, feeling the blue of my lips, the deep blue of my fingers.

"No," I say again. "Harder."

We lay still, caught inside each other for a long time. It might have been hours. I don't know because it's summer and there are no clocks anywhere. Through the front windshield, I can see a few stars and the hemlock branches weeping over us. Ray hears a noise, footsteps, and I know what it is even before he whispers the words, a tiny shock wave passing out through his chest and arrowing into mine.

A car slows alongside us, and the door creaks open. There's a face at the window. Only I see it, and then it's gone. A man's voice says *kids courting*. The car pulls off up Peachtree Battle.

It might be minutes or hours later that Elijah Johnson looks in the window on the passenger side. He stands there a long time, looks at our bodies together, at me, at my open eyes. He presses one fingertip against the glass and I try to think what he means. I can tell by his breathing Ray is awake. There's nothing to do but keep still. Right now all three of us know every single thing the other knows.

132

Elijah Johnson checks all the doors and finds them locked. He looks in at us again, then he starts to whistle. He walks off down the street, whistling a song he might have made up then and there. It's tuneless, high and sad. He keeps whistling so that we'll know when he's far, far away.

In bed that night I touch the places where Ray's imprinted his body onto mine and I hear that whistling again, deep and sad as a cry. It's not a boy this time, but a train headed south and west. I picture myself drifting with that train, not asleep in a seat, but a stowaway holding Sam on my back, lying flat on top of a boxcar or riding the rails underneath, the metal and wood splintering my body, the diesel howl so deafening that ahead and behind I see a trail of skulls, the whitened remains of nightwatchmen and other sleepless creatures. I'm praying this train will never stop, I'm praying to disappear and I lie on my back watching out the window while the sky undoes itself over this town, opening up its own heart right over my head, so that the blood falls on my face like light.

Elijah

HE don't ever fight back or cover his face neither, and he don't say a word. My fist go into his skin like it's to pull something out and his bones moves backward out the other side.

I ain't going after him no more. I might keep laying for him and watching to see where he go, but I ain't going to touch him.

I don't need to. Sometimes at night I believe I can still feel his skin and his bones cracking across the back of my hand. His skin is always warm at the touch, like putting your fist into a tub of water, down till it finds the bottom. I can remember the way he fall into my arms and hang there till I move back and he drop to his knees then all the way down to where his hands is holding onto my legs like somebody begging you not to go on and leave them. Do anything, that voice is saying, only just stay.

Ray

THE thing is, after he left, I was gone too, and that's why I have to find him. I lost my memory some and while Mother and Noreen were thinking back, *What did he say? Did he ever mention it? Did he tell you?* there wasn't much I could remember so I had to go on ahead out the door after him. My memory's come back to me some but mostly there's only this minute that I'm talking in now and the minute that will come next. After that, nothing. One of those stories I never understood in school, everything is *nada. Our father who art in nada.* Now I get it. This is that same story.

"Ray," Buddy said that night out by the dumpster, "what wants to be found gets found, and your daddy won't be found. I could name you all the ones I heard of this summer won't be found either."

He said that to me and he kept right on talking, naming the lost daddies he knew about. The only way I could think of to make him stop was to punch him in, like he was a TV you can't turn off any other way. I heard of a girl who did that. She didn't like what she was hearing on the news and kicked in her television. She had on cowboy boots.

I knew I'd only have to hit him once. It doesn't take much to put out a lie. Now if he was telling the truth, well, I could've broken every bone in his body and he would've kept right on talking. Still I didn't mean for things to turn out the way they have. It's not my fault but it kind of is. If it wasn't for me, he probably wouldn't even have been out that day, never mind walking home from the clinic by himself with his eyes swollen almost shut.

I didn't bargain on Elijah but I didn't not bargain on him either. It's an eye for an eye in this world and I know it. He'll come after me out of the shadows, and then I won't even feel the pain. What I feel is the quiet lying heavy over us. There's never any sound except my breathing and his, and after a while I can't hear that either.

People keep asking me what I'm going to do now but I don't know what they mean. When is now? Is it after Daddy left or before he comes back? Is it before Buddy or after? Robbie Lynn is now, but it seems like with her pictures all over the place, she's everybody's now. Maybe I'll go into antiques with Joe when he gets to town, start up a business down here. Maybe I'll go to night school and learn how to be night. Right now I'm shooting targets with a single-action army that was Daddy's. I use moonpies mostly, stand them up on the back fence and aim right for their little moonpie hearts.

He used to go on trips all the time, so maybe this is one of those. He'd take us with him when he could, both me and Noreen. He took me by myself to Chicago for a month the winter I was eight. He didn't mean for us to stay a month, but his business went on and on. Lake Michigan was frozen, and when he was gone during the day I'd sneak out of the hotel and walk on the ice, just far enough I told myself to see the badlands in Alberta. Once I helped save a woman who'd fallen through, talking to her until emergency rescue came. I told her just what she needed to hear, whispered it into her ear, my lips going blue where they touched her skin. He'd leave me alone in that hotel for days and I used to imagine what would happen if I fell through the ice and my body drifted away through the locks into Lake Huron and he came back and found me gone.

On the days it was too windy to go out, I'd ask at the hotel desk for postcards of the Wrigley Building, the Lake, the John Hancock Building. Back upstairs, I'd write long letters to Mother and Noreen and enclose the postcards with us drawn in. I'd tell them we'd just been doing some very interesting things, spelling the words out carefully, and now we were resting, but soon we'd do more. Daddy would take these letters and mail them in the morning, at least that's what I thought. Three years ago, I found them all, never even stamped, stacked on his closet shelf.

Later on, when Noreen loved horses, he took her all over to see the Clydesdales and the steeplechase and the Lippizan stallions. Her room was so full of their statues there was hardly any space in it for her.

Then he promised to take Noreen and me to Puerto Rico. It was for winning prizes at school, he said, a few weeks before Honors Day. I was going to win most improved and Noreen would get best all-around. I got my prize but best all-around went to somebody else, not Noreen. I remember her face, round like the moon and pale white, standing up onstage with the choir singing the last song before the benediction. I could see her thinking there are no more prizes, there are no more prizes while the music rose and rose and her voice dropped against it down to a whisper. *I am bounding toward my God and my reward,* she sang. I could see her imagining the golden beaches of San Juan drifting farther and farther away from her.

The morning of the day we were supposed to leave, she came into my bedroom, shut the door, and handed me five dollars in quarters, dimes, and nickels. She was crying and her face was red and dirty with the tears and with her trying to hide them. Buy me something nice. Buy me a necklace of shells, she said.

She and my mother drove us to the airport and walked us out to the gate. We all kissed good-bye and then Daddy took Noreen's hand and pulled so hard she almost fell down. Surprise, he said, surprise. Momma was smiling, waving good-bye to the three of us. I don't have any clothes, Noreen said. We'll buy them there, Daddy told her. New. Everything new.

In San Juan, we stayed on the beach in a big hotel with gardens for the lobby. We got lost in them every morning on our way to breakfast and only the smell of bacon and cooked fish got us found again. Daddy would leave us early in the morning to do his business and come back late at night, sometimes long after we'd gotten tired of laughing at the Spanish language channels on TV and fallen asleep. He'd order up beers and stand out on the balcony drinking them. He slept out there too, in his clothes, sometimes stretched along the bottom railing like he was trying to get under it and drop down into the ocean. In the morning, he'd leave again right after breakfast.

Noreen and I played out on the beach and inside at the laundry equipment convention in the hotel ballroom. We collected free no-iron napkins in twelve colors, tiny soaps, memo pads, and plastic ballpoint pens. In the hotel gift shop, we bought shell necklaces for Momma and later I secretly bought another one for Robbie Lynn. Daddy rented face masks and snorkels for us and we spent the whole day floating on our stomachs, looking into the blue water, drifting farther out to where the bottom dropped off and only dark blind fish swam below us. We never saw a single one, but we'd make up the shapes and colors to tell Daddy when he came back to the hotel that night.

By four in the afternoon our backs were raw with sunburn, the skin beginning to crinkle in on itself. We got ourselves doused with Solarcaine then lay on the two big beds in the hotel room, drifting in and out of fever and dozing. Noreen called out for Daddy in her sleep, *Where is he?* insisting like she was awake and wanted some kind of answer. When I said he's not here, I saw a tear run out of her closed eye and drop off the side of her nose.

The next day was Sunday and he stayed at the hotel with us. After breakfast he said we should all three swim out into the ocean as far as we could go, just to do it. Noreen said she would wait for us on the beach, but he said no, we'd all have to go. All three of us, as far as we could, until we couldn't swim any farther. Then what, Noreen said. You'll see, Daddy told us, it's not far to Cuba or even back to Florida.

There'd been rain the night before and it washed in blood-red seaweed that churned and foamed around our ankles. We held Daddy's hands and picked our way through it, skipping out high and splashing to hide that we were more afraid than we'd ever been in our lives. Even after I couldn't touch bottom and Noreen couldn't, he kept walking, holding our hands, then swimming out, back towards Florida, he said, telling us not to struggle, but rise and drop with the waves.

A lifeguard blew his whistle and called us back. Daddy let go my hand, turned and waved, then faced back out to sea. We heard the whistle again, and Daddy just laughed. I was very tired. I can't, I told him. Yes you can, he said.

Noreen went into the next wave instead of over it and got a mouthful of sea water. Careful, Daddy said. We still have a ways to get to Miami Beach, he said.

I don't remember anything after that until I was lying in the bottom of a motorboat. Noreen was sitting up and coughing. Daddy was talking about undertow. His face was turned away from us, looking south. What a pull, he said, I never dreamed. Back in our room that night, he sat outside on the balcony drinking bloody marys and naming the constellations he could recognize, both Dippers, the Seven Sisters, Cassiopeia's Chair, Orion, who was always his favorite. Noreen and I fell asleep, sleep like waves moving under us. When we woke up, it was Monday morning and he was gone.

Now Mr. Hamilton next door is leaving for work so I guess I've stayed up all night this time. I hope you and Buddy Johnson are out there dreaming the name of every star you know, the list that's kept you safe all your life, wherever you were, walking downtown or swimming in water with currents full of drowning shadows that look like yours.

It's the edge of that same kind of water you've brought me down to now, my eyes wide open like I'm looking underwater through Momma's lace curtains to where the sky's pulling itself back and the whole world stands naked and there's nowhere you can hide.

Gus

JOE Ithaca gets to the Greshams' early Saturday morning. He's driven straight from Vermont, eighteen hours in a blue Malibu with pink showing through on top where the paint's worn away. He's tall and solid with sharp features like Ray's, but swarthy instead of pale like milk. He wears his hair in a ponytail that just barely makes it, some of the shorter pieces falling over his good eye so all you see is the patch over the other. Ray says when he takes the patch off, it's just skin, pale and soft, like there never was an eye there at all.

In the Greshams' driveway, we can't keep from staring, and it makes him shy.

"Will one of y'all sign for this," he says pointing at his own chest, "and then direct me to a bed?"

You can hear that Joe Ithaca isn't from Vermont or even from Ithaca and later that evening he tells us he comes from Richmond, where Mrs. Gresham grew up and Noreen and Ray's daddy went to the University. They're sitting at either end of the kitchen table talking while we listen. Mrs. Gresham pours herself a drink, puts the bottle of bourbon on the lazy susan, and spins it toward Joe. I swear she hasn't said this much in all the years I've known Noreen and been coming over to this house, and I keep trying to catch Noreen's eye but she's not paying any attention to me. You can see how her whole body is listening to her mother and Joe Ithaca go through friends of friends, street names, old college stories. Joe's father is a professor emeritus of classics.

"He never took any classics that I remember," Mrs. Gresham says. "He had a hard enough time with the live languages, and after a while all he wanted to do was leave, so we did, in the dead of night right after graduation. Like to make your head spin. I enjoyed it there though, tradition everywhere you went. And hospitals. I've never been in a town with so many hospitals. Great place to get sick."

"My mother's a nurse at the VA Hospital."

"So your folks are still there?"

"They'll be there until they die."

"Well it's a good place for that."

"Dying?" Joe says. "I'm with you on that one."

"No, I meant retiring."

Mrs. Gresham looks like she's not sure if she's supposed to laugh. She tips her head way back and swallows the last of the bourbon in her glass. Joe reaches across the table and turns the lazy susan toward her. He waits while she pours a refill and spins it back toward himself.

"I have to defend the place," she says. "My husband got a decent education. You could have too, you know, with your daddy teaching there and all. All you had to do probably was just walk across Cary Street to get a decent education."

"No ma'am I couldn't," Joe says. "It wouldn't have worked out. For one thing my number came up. My father was already protesting the war and he wanted me to be a conscientious objector or head out to Canada like my brothers, but I wanted to go. For a while I believed in what was happening over there and then that turned into just wanting to get the whole mess cleaned up. So I told him okay, I'd take off for Canada, but I stopped a little short of the border, hung around for a while in Ithaca, New York and dreamed up my new name. Then I went, first to Fort Hamilton, then all the way over. This was 1969. I was over there three years doing clean up, and I've been in Burlington ever since I got back."

"Don't you see your parents?" Robbie Lynn asks, which is just what I was wondering.

"My father told me not to come home, but I talk to my mother."

"What was it like?" Mrs. Gresham asks.

"What?"

"Being over there, in Vietnam, what was it like?"

"It wasn't like anything. I don't talk about it anymore. I get tired of the sound of my own voice."

"Well, I admire you. It was noble, even if it was a damn shambles. You're part of a real piece of history."

"No ma'am," Joe says, "not noble and not real. Rainy. A rainy piece of history. That about describes it."

"But you said you went to clean up. To my mind that's noble."

"It would seem that way, yes it would, but I'll tell you something, with all due respect as you're my hostess here and try as I might to get shut of them, I've still got my manners, that's a load of horse shit they feed you about noble. Defeat is defeat. Having the shit kicked out of you isn't pretty or romantic and you sure as hell don't want to go around talking about it all the time."

Joe stops and looks around the table, then rests his eye on Mrs. Gresham. He spins the lazy susan back around to her.

"I can see," he says, "that your glass is empty and your heart is full."

"It is," she says, getting up from the table, "and I'm tired." She glances over at Ray but Joe keeps his eye fixed on her. "But I'm glad you're here."

"I go where I'm needed, ma'am," he says.

At midnight we're still sitting in the kitchen listening to Joe's stories and playing rummy even though there's too many with Noreen and me, Robbie Lynn and Ray. We're drinking black coffee because Joe is and eating sweet rolls frozen in the middle. When I shuffle with one hand the way Grandma taught me, it gets quiet around the table and then Joe casts his eye over at me and says I remind him of a girl he knew in Richmond. She

151

had hair like mine, black but shifting to blue in certain kinds of light. He says I move the way she did too, like with every step I'm changing my mind.

"She was always daring boys to fall in love with her, so most of them backed way off. I don't know where she is now. I keep looking for her in Burlington, thinking maybe who knows. I have this idea that someday she'll come into the store with a piece of that puke-green wedgewood and say something like do you have the other one to this set? And I'll say darling, don't you think that's the ugliest fucking color you've ever seen? And she'll say Joe, it's you. I'd know that mouth of yours anywhere."

I have to tell you something here, and it's that I think I was falling in love with him from then on. So now I've said it. When he drives Noreen and Robbie Lynn and me out to the river to see the place where we found the body, I sit up front next to him and keep my eyes straight ahead and read off the names of streets, but I'm watching him just the same. You can do that, watch somebody by feeling them move and talk, the way a blind person does. We tell him about Buddy Johnson and I recite the names of the missing children.

"I like to keep track," I tell him.

"I know," he says, and I believe he does know. All this time driving with him, getting him coffee when he comes into the Brookwood, I've been thinking what if he could be you come back from the dead? I know it's crazy but I can't help myself. There's a part of me that believes all Noreen's talk about lost shall be found.

Noreen

IN *the name of the Father*, that's how the Monsignor begins at high noon, pressing his thumb and first finger together and drawing them in clean lines down his face to where the breastbone ends, and across his shoulders, left to right, so hard and sharp I expect someday he'll fall apart into four neat hunks of flesh and all will be revealed, down to the quick and the dead.

I try to sit towards the back, but it doesn't make any difference, I can't escape, and on his way up the aisle, the Monsignor will tap me on the shoulder and ask me to read the first lesson and the psalm. *They're marked for you*, he says, and when I go up to the lectern, there's a green ribbon in the Holy Bible, and that's how I know. In the winter, red and blue light from the side windows shines directly on the page and on your hands as you hold them steady on the bottom margin. In the summer, today for instance, the light's dropped to the floor in front of the lectern where you can get a good look at it while you're reading. The picture in the window is clearer in summer, the faces of the four evangelists reflected to look like they're riding on each other's shoulders, Matthew on Mark on Luke on John. It reminds me of a circus act I saw at the Civic Center a long time ago, the Amazing Fiumi Brothers, four of them big as horses, tossing sticks of fire and juggling knives. At the end, they made the Human Obelisk by jumping up on each other's shoulders. The last two used a trampoline to get high enough. It's how they'll get to heaven someday, the ringmaster said, climbing and climbing, finally Pietro pulling Guiseppe up into clouds.

155

At the noon Mass, there's no singing or music and usually only ten of us, give or take. I recognize everybody but don't know their names except one, a lady named Clare, thin and graceful, moving in front of the lectern like to remind you of a stem of river grass. Most days she reads the second lesson. I have to close my eyes when she starts because I can hardly stand the sight of her face, it's so beautiful. She looks to be filled up with holy light and her mouth trembles over every word like she's about to cry. When it comes time for special intentions, she always prays for the missing children. She asks God to make them so heavy they can't be lifted out of their homes or up off the streets. *Give our children the great weight of divine love.* I've heard her say she keeps track of them the same way Gus does. Sometimes I think Clare is what Gus could be if she ever stopped hating God for taking Billy Marsh away from her.

Today it's warm and close in church and I can barely rise from the pew to go up and find the green ribbon in Ezekiel. The heat makes me start to take the words differently, looking at them for signs like Robbie or Gus would. *As I looked, behold, a strong wind came out of the north, and a great cloud with brightness round about it, and fire flashing forth continually, and in the midst of the fire came a likeness of four living creatures.*

This heaviness is in me because I know where my father has gone. I know it, I swear. He's gone to Clarksville, Tennessee where he's going to pick up a racehorse called Malicious Music. He showed me the bill of sale and the silks, yellow with a black checkerboard. The jockey's name is Little Richard, and I've been carrying his phone number in my wallet. I've called twice and both times he says there's nobody he knows now or ever has known named Willis Gresham.

Their legs were straight, and the soles of their feet were like the soles of a calf's foot; and they sparkled like burnished bronze. Under their wings on their four sides they had human hands.

He said he was going to bring Malicious Music back and run her in the steeplechases. I knew by the way he said it he was lying. He wouldn't look me in the eye and he rattled the change in his pockets so it was louder than his voice.

And the four had their faces and their wings thus: their wings touched one another, they went every one straight forward, without turning as they went. As for the likeness of their faces, each had the face of a man in front; the four had the face of a lion on the right side, the four had the face of an ox on the left side, and the four had the face of an eagle at the back. Such were their faces. And their wings were spread out above; each creature had two wings, each of which touched the wing of another, while two covered their bodies. And each went straight forward; wherever the spirit would go, they went, without turning as they went.

I know all this and still I keep it to myself. Some days I think of telling Momma, just to get out from under the weight of the knowing, but I can't predict how she'd act. I could tell Joe Ithaca but then he'd go up to Clarksville. He'd tell Ray and they'd go just like that, and I know how it would be with Ray and Daddy once they got there. I know there'd be words and maybe worse than that. They're just alike and when Daddy goes after Ray you can see how it's like a man wanting to fight with his own soul and punish himself for the evil he's done. It'd be worse now because Ray's going around courting trouble. He's got this look about him these days, the right side of his face all bruised and swollen, reddish purple like a birthmark. His right eye's swelled nearly shut and it makes him hold his head with his neck stretched out and off the right some so his good eye can do most of the work. With his arm and shoulder bound up that way, it's like he's set to block a punch or getting ready to throw one, you can't tell which. Joe too, he's got a dangerous air to him with that lost eye, buried somewhere in a field on the other side of the world, full of all the sights it's seen.

In the midst of the living creatures there was something that looked like burning coals of fire, like torches moving to and fro among the living creatures; and the fire was bright and out of the fire went forth lightning. And the living creatures darted to and fro like a flash of lightning.

I could tell Gus, or Elbert and Ross. I could tell them and they'd keep it secret until I figured out what to do.

I could go to Clarksville myself, but I'm scared to. I know just what would happen. First he'd hate me being there, but then I'd get to be his Precious again, and he'd say here's a horse you can have for your own and what do you think of that? I'd say no Daddy I don't want a horse now, just come on home, and he'd say let's have some supper and you'll feel different.

If it was like when we saw the Lippizan stallions, we'd get dressed up, him in a brown suit and me in a dress, usually new, bought that very day. He never liked the clothes Momma packed for me. They were ordinary, he said, like any other little girl's. I was marked, he said, marked for life, as he picked out ruffles and petticoats, lace anklets and black patent leather shoes to match.

We'd go to big crowded restaurants and the waiters would form a ring around our table and watch me until I finished with a bowl or a plate or a glass of water, and then they'd lean in from their places to take away whatever it was and bring me something new. It was their own complicated dance and they were doing it to music only they could hear.

After dinner, we'd go to other places, darker and smaller, where he'd leave me at the bar, high up on a stool where I couldn't get down or even turn around without falling or getting dizzy. I'd have something sweet to drink, jewel-colored, red or gold, and the bartender would keep close by but without talking. Two or three times, Daddy'd come back to the bar with some of his friends to introduce me and they'd want hugs and kisses, but their faces were so big and greasy, scratchy like buttered toast. I couldn't stand how they'd look at me, how their eyes would roll in their heads when they'd laugh. I'd lay my head on the bar and cry I hate it, I hate it, but they loved that too.

Now as I looked at the living creatures, I saw a wheel upon the earth beside them, one for each of the four. As for the appearance of these wheels and their construction: their appearance was like the

gleaming of a chrysolite, and the four had the same likeness, their con-
struction being as it were a wheel within a wheel. The four wheels had
rims and they had spokes, and their rims were full of eyes round about.

I believe Robbie Lynn's parents are in heaven and all the little murdered children are in heaven and Billy Marsh is probably there too, and I can feel them all looking down on me and waiting to see what I'm going to do. Their eyes come loose from their bodies and walk over my skin like spiders, across every inch, trying to find a deep place to get inside and watch my heart. There's plenty of room for all of them because I'm dead empty inside. If your heart's a bone, then mine's dry and white with no marrow left, and if it's a fist like they say, then mine's knuckled up and blue with cold.

I lead the psalm, but I'm not even hearing myself. My mother's just come in the back door of the church and she's standing still in the center aisle beside the last pew. She starts to make the sign of the cross over herself, but then she hears it's me reading so she stops and her arms fall to her sides. Her feet are exactly together as if she's about to come down the aisle, and now in a flash I can see her holding herself this same way just before she's going to walk down the aisle to be married to Daddy. She's wearing her white eyelet wedding gown that I've heard of but never seen except in the pictures, and her right arm is holding her own daddy's arm. She's about to float up this aisle toward Daddy and the priest, and she doesn't know the future and she doesn't dream there's any sadness to come.

What are you thinking Momma, I want to ask her, but she's so far away. If I could only get into that dress myself maybe I would know, that dress or any of her cotillion dresses stacked in boxes up in the attic.

I finish the psalm and go to sit down next to the Monsignor, but I can still feel them behind me, Mother and the ghost of her daddy, whose eyes disappeared when he smiled, coming relentlessly on up the aisle, nearer and nearer while Clare stands at the lectern reading from the Book of Revelation. It's too much, her voice, that light pouring forth from her face when she tells us all about the seven seals, the white horse, the red horse, the black horse, the pale horse with its rider whose name is death.

Joe Ithaca

LIKE I said to Sidney Gresham, I go where I'm needed. This trip's mostly for Ray though. He's a youngster, but he's been a good friend this past year, like a son if I'm imagining it right. He said that to me once, and I had to admit it was true, I do want him to be my son on some days of the week.

Two times I was with Ray I remember real clear. One was the first morning we went out after I gave him his gun. It was already light, too light for deer, so we went into the scrub after birds, combing the opposite sides of a hedgerow. I knew we wouldn't get anything, but it didn't matter because what I really wanted to do was watch Ray work his gun, load it and unload it, tuck it under his arm or up against his shoulder. From twenty yards away, I couldn't see how his eyes were moving, but every so often he'd turn his head and listen, hold his breath so he became neither man nor beast, but something not of this world.

Then there was the first morning we went to hunt deer. Something got into Ray, I don't know what, but he kept to a dead silence the whole ride in. When we'd hiked into the woods and set up, he didn't want to load his gun. I couldn't tell what it was all about and I sure as hell wasn't going to have a goddamn discussion about it right then. I figured he must've had words with his girl back home, and I let it drop.

He explained it to me on the way back to Burlington. I didn't get it all then, and I still don't think I do, but it seems that in the night before we went out he started to think of this girl of his as a deer, her body white in places, but still brown from the

163

summer, her eyes that black glass hunters say would throw your own soul back at you if you could ever get close enough. She was skittish the way deer get, but curious too, strong-legged and graceful. I may be embellishing some here because all this talk got me tranced. Then I thought maybe the kid had found some mighty fine weed I didn't know of and I was on the verge of asking him to let me in on it when something in my gut went weak, and I knew it was for real. I knew it wasn't Ray's talk getting me tranced, but that girl talking through him, and when I got down to Atlanta and saw her, I knew I was right.

She's sure a beauty, and there is something deerish about her. All three of those girls are, the stuff that makes civilizations rise and fall. To see them there that first morning in Ray's driveway, it was something else, those girls in their shorts cut high off their thighs, tanned and talking the way they do. Mr. Ithaca, it was. Hell, that ain't even my real name and it sounds like some damn hallelujah chorus coming out of those sweet mouths. It's good to be with girls. It heals you. If it weren't for them, who else would we have to love?

So I've been here awhile now, helping out at the Parents' Task Force and getting up ball games at the kids' camp. Nobody much trusted me at first. I knew it would be that way and I'd just have to ride it out. It's the eye. Some guys it makes seem dignified but not me. The girls would go with me at first and that softened my look some. That's another thing girls can do for you if you let them.

Like I said, I came here to help Ray out, calm him down, get him off the streets at night, but these missing kids are tearing me up inside. It gets to be you see a kid out on the street and you want to ask where they're going or follow them to make sure they're okay. Even the white kids. Nobody really knows. A couple of nights, I've dreamed about finding all of them hidden in a cave or living together in the woods, splashing in the river. In the room where I'm sleeping at the Greshams', there's pictures of Ray's dad when he was a boy, and his face gets into my dreams too.

164

I wake up in a sweat and I think how bad I want to find the fucker who's doing this to these kids, and make him suffer. Everybody feels the same way but they act it out a little differently. I rage out loud, Ray's sister Noreen prays for them in church, goes around hungry, and does these mystery novenas like she's got some secret message from on high. Robbie Lynn cries when she reads about them in the paper, but I have a notion it's tears for her folks too. Gus keeps a list of the boys' names, and the dates of their disappearances.

To me, she's the mystery, Gus is. Robbie Lynn you can chart because you just decide what a regular eighteen-year-old girl would do or say or act like and she's the opposite. Gus is shaky territory. She'll be carrying around some big old fat book to read and talk her fine talk, but then she'll sit beside you in the car, read all the road signs to you, and twist her hair into knots the way a five-year-old kid would. I think about her too much. It scares me. I got eleven years on her, several entire worlds and lifetimes to go with them, and still my chest goes tight when I see her. She reminds me of a girl I knew, but it isn't that. She makes me feel like somebody's hero.

She talks about this boy who was struck by lightning last summer. She won't tell the story of it all at once straight through, but it comes out in bits and pieces and it gets in my head like a picture and stays there. I can see them clear as anything just the way she said, out on Lake Lanier by seven that morning, put in a ways off from the pleasure boaters, and I've memorized the names she told me, Buford Dam, New Holland, Flowery Branch. They were following a hydrographic map she said and looking for sunken islands under the eelgrass and tobacco cabbage.

He said to her *Try to keep the fish in the water while you take the hook out. You'd think it's so they'll stay wet and breathing, but it's not. What gets them is gravity. It's a real shock.*

As the morning haze burned off a different kind of haze replaced it. At ten the sky was still overcast and the color of the

165

water deepened to olive. Over the side of the canoe it made a perfect mirror. If she looked at her own face then, she saw it without flaws, her eyes like entryways into the lake's deepest parts. She told him it was going to rain and asked if they should head in.

He said they should. He said if it's an all-day storm they weren't going to like sitting under a tarp for eight hours.

If she's the girl I think she is, she gave him a look then that might have made him weak in the knees.

Sometimes it's like I've never seen you before, like I'm still seeing you for the first time.

He asked her then if she saw them getting married someday and she said she didn't know.

I think I'd like to.

Then he talked about his mother and father, who never married, each other or anybody else.

I remember one night in the winter in Maine, I was a kid, maybe five or six, and my mother and me, we'd been snowed in for three days. All of a sudden the front door burst open and there he was, my father, laughing, shaking snow off himself, stamping his feet. He stormed into the house, pulled my mother off the couch and danced her around the living room. It got quiet, then she picked me up and the three of us kept dancing.

Off in the distance there was a clap of thunder and just over his shoulder she saw lightning fork its way down the sky. Rain splattered into the boat.

Thunderstorm. That's good, it'll move the fish some.

He could tell she was nervous so he kept talking.

He was gone a lot but he was always in the air. She'd talk about him, show me pictures, give me stuff that was his. And then he'd come back.

Another flash of lightning, much brighter. She counted to herself between it and the thunder. Billy handed her a piece of tarp and she wrapped it around her shoulders.

He'd come back for a week or two and it would be like a holiday.

The rain was slanting in at them, nearly horizontal. Other boats were heading for the dock at Buford Dam, and the sight of them calmed her some.

Now he's with her all the time.

I can make up the rest because I've seen guys blown apart this way, up real close and personal. There was probably a flash between them in the boat and she was thrown backward into the bow on top of the life preservers. Billy's tee shirt on his left side caught fire and smoke rose off his shoulder. His hair stood straight up away from his head and the left side of his face caved in and turned black. His right eye opened wide and he made a screeching cry that was the last thing he'd ever say and then he slumped over the side of the boat, almost into the water.

She tried to crawl to him but the boat was going in circles. She probably called his name, hearing herself from far off like she was out in the water instead of four feet away. She was telling him to stay where he was, not to move until she could get there and then she was there pulling herself up on his knees, reaching under his left side where she found nothing but a wet gob of shirt and burnt skin to hold on to.

She told me a man and a woman in a motorboat pulled in beside them. The woman tried to steer in close while the man lifted Billy's left leg and dragged him into their boat. The woman took off her terry cloth robe and tucked it around Billy's shoulders and over his knees. Gus kept talking to him, telling him he was going to be all right. He stared at her with one open eye.

At the dock, people helped carry him into the tackle shop and they laid him down on a blanket. She said it seemed like a long time before an ambulance came and when it finally did, and the paramedics tried to revive him by breathing into his mouth and massaging his heart, they couldn't. When it looked like they were giving up, Gus told them to keep going, not to stop, he can make it, she said, he's so strong, and when they shook their heads, she tried to press on his heart and breathe into his mouth until one of them pulled her away, saying no honey, he was already gone when you first touched his shoulder back there on the lake.

Later she probably tried to think of what had to be done first, carrying the list around in her head like a piece of rope with knots in it she had to untie. Then she was back in school. Everyone was good to her, she said, they let her alone. She felt like he was with her all the time.

Robbie Lynn

EVERYBODY who can

drives down to the river for the fireworks and you go in daylight so people can see you and so it's still safe to swim if you care about that. If you ran in the road race this morning you stay in your shorts and wear the tee shirt everybody gets or maybe even keep on your race number if it's low enough to brag about. Or if you're a girl you want everybody to see how you did up your red white and blue this year and still left most of yourself bare.

The younger girls walk slowly around the edges of the parking lot in threes and fours facing in different directions but their eyes stay blank and their faces don't give anything away. Then some news will come to one of them, borne on the air or seen with those eyes that don't look like they're being used at all, and she'll whisper it to her friends and they'll all laugh with their eyes piercing deep into each other's so that anyone watching them will feel unspeakably sad and alone.

Gus and Noreen and I used to be this way but now we're the older girls who walk by themselves down through the middles of parking lots, crosshatching between cars and families with their picnics spread in backseats or sometimes down on the asphalt below the front bumper. We move toward cars where there's music playing out of the open windows and doors. It might be somebody we know but more than that, the music gives us a way to walk. When you move in the direction of music, another kind of force takes over that's not muscles and not bones and not even blood, though that's what people sometimes take it for.

One by one tonight we walk back up from the river, winding through the parking lot to Noreen's car where Gus left the second blanket, Noreen left her set of dry clothes, and I was supposed to meet Ray. Always we go alone and come back alone and even with Ray I keep us a distance apart. When I hear his breathing too close behind me, I move out ahead or turn between two cars where he wouldn't expect me to turn, where the bumpers are pulled up so close we have to pass through one at a time.

All around are the radios and the voices and the bodies whose sunburn makes them tired and electric at the same time. As I pass by, I put on the music like it's clothes.

Down by the water's edge, Joe Ithaca and Noreen are sitting on either side of the cooler and talking quietly without looking at each other. Gus has just walked off by herself, I can see her white shirt twenty yards off, moving in the direction of the Paces Ferry bridge. Noreen looks like she's about to cry.

"You can't even have a conversation with her anymore," she says.

"Gus?" I say.

"We aren't like we used to be."

I tell her nobody is.

"What did you say to her?" Ray asks.

Noreen cuts her eyes at Joe.

"It was before any of you got down here. I said she shouldn't think so much about somebody who's dead."

"Jesus, Noreen," Ray shakes his head. "What did she say?"

"She said 'You do.'"

At first I can't think what Gus would have meant, but Ray says it again, *Jesus*, and then I know.

Darkness comes on full and deep and the fireworks start up before Gus gets back. She walks up from behind and sits down beside Noreen. I watch Noreen slowly move her body so her shoulders dip toward Gus. They hold their faces up to the sky at exactly the same angle and they laugh at the grand finale, then look at each other, but it's too dark to tell what's passing between them.

When the lights from the American flag have dripped all the way out of the sky and we're left in darkness, Joe asks Gus how she ever found her way back to us and she said it wasn't hard because the fireworks lit us up pretty well. It was one of the most beautiful sights she ever looked on, from ten feet away all of us lit up like we were on fire, like we'd swallowed the fireworks and they were burning us from the inside out.

Gus

THIS is where you and I used to hike down to swim at night, and still every time Noreen and Robbie Lynn bring me here I think you might come back and every time we leave it feels like I've left you standing by yourself in the water knee-deep and your arms held open because I've just walked out of them. You're right there behind Noreen and Robbie with that last look of surprise on your face. I wonder if either of us might have left something here in the kudzu. Maybe I could find it right now, a button, a penny, a pencil fallen out of your pocket. My feet move in circles over the ground feeling their way along. What did you carry in your pockets? I'm trying to think. The penknife I gave you, spare change.

You can tell your children.

I can tell my children what?

You can tell them you never had to carry spare change when you went out with their father.

I can't remember what else. It seems like a long time ago.

Nearly a whole year later I'm dreaming it this way. We're in the Boston Whaler, you and me, not the canoe, but there's that same storm come up suddenly on the lake. You're standing in the boat with your back to me and then you turn around and you say *Do you dance?* and I'm in your arms. There's a band playing "Waltz Across Texas" and you're kissing the top of my head. The left side of your face is blackened and sooty from the lightning bolt but if I'd known better I might have mistook that darkness for shadow.

Then it's another night, later and warm until we start moving fast on your motorcycle and I get that ripple of chill up under my tee shirt and by then it's too late to stop. There's nowhere to go back to for a jacket, I've got to ride it out, try not to think about gooseflesh rising on my bare arms, the way slowing down and turning corners makes it feel like the bike's kicking up dust, dust rising up my arms, over my shoulders, and in a minute, I'll be breathing it, tasting dust, choking on it.

It's the night before you'll be struck by lightning on Lake Lanier. I know this now. It's two weeks before summer ends and we start back to school. I know this too, but none of it helps one single bit.

I'm wearing a tee shirt that's been cut off and won't tuck into my jeans so it's blowing up in the back, flapping its ragged hem at the cars behind us. I can feel my nipples going hard in the cold, and I lean into your back, thinking you'd like the feel of that, thinking it would be a way to say all the things this night and speeding on a dark road won't let me say.

We're not wearing helmets and your hair whips back at me, snapping hard and sharp at my mouth. Strands of hair catch in my eyes and at the same time a sentence spins itself out in my head, one word at a time, *I deserve this*, my own voice inside the dark tunnel of my head, *I deserve this*, slowly like I'm explaining it to someone. I don't pull my face away but rest my chin more firmly on your shoulder. I see my reflection in the left side mirror and then a flash of streetlight into the whites of your eyes. You look only at the road.

On Mount Paran, the air temperature changes, warm to cold to warm again. I wonder why this happens and I tell myself I'll ask you later but I never do. Back and forth, warm to cold, *he loves me he loves me not*. I don't know why I do such things, ride without a helmet, love a boy this way. We take a right on Northside Parkway, ride for a quarter mile then swing in toward the back gate of the high school. We've come to find out it's pure chance, some nights the gate is locked, some nights not.

Tonight we're in luck. Through the parking lot, there's a dirt path leading out to the track and the football field. You park the bike behind the scoreboard posts, and then we follow a steeper path down to the river. Even in the shallows, even after a day when the temperature's hit a hundred degrees, the water is still cool. The current runs strong here, so we don't get too far out, just to our knees, still wearing our sneakers and all our clothes.

"River rats," you say, "watch out."

The water smells like my bath after I get out of it.

"Billy," I say, moving into your arms.

You hold me with one arm over my face, over my ears so I can hear your heartbeat. My face drops against your chest and you kiss the top of my head. We stand still this way while the river moves against our legs. Somewhere up north, the stars are falling into the water so that down here it's cool and sharp and filled with the memory of light.

Billy Marsh

FOR nearly a year after, Gus has been writing me postcards. She'll write the message, sign her name, then tear it up or throw it into whatever moving body of water she happens to be near. She watches them float awhile, then cave in on themselves and disappear under water. In the right light, at five in the afternoon, their glossy finish catches the sun and they come to look like fish, bass or bream swimming too far inland and going belly up before you have a chance to bait your hook, play out the line, and feel the pull of what's already gone under.

She tells me about the soothsayers, the mediums, and their tarot cards coming up hanged man, drowned man. She says that's how bad it's getting, the city willing to try just about anything to find out who's taking those children and dumping them in the woods or in the river. There's a palm reader from New Jersey who says she's been called to contact the children's spirits, and she's heard them all right, their wispy voices trying to tell her their secrets, crying in the dark for their mommas. She leaves sugar babies in the front yard of the Governor's Mansion, and at night the little black ghosts come to hunt for them. In the morning the grass is trampled and their tears are everywhere.

The count is up to fourteen bodies, she tells me, sixteen children missing. One boy was last seen when his step-brother dropped him off at a shopping center where he was going to sell cans of air freshener. Buddy Johnson was on his way home from the free clinic on Auburn Avenue where the doctor said he was healing up just fine.

Hundreds of police officers and volunteers conduct Saturday searches over wooded areas in Fulton County.

Eleven o'clock curfew for children under sixteen.

Two skeletons found in southwest Fulton County. Teeth used as the basis for identification. Police accuse the FBI and crime lab technicians of mishandling evidence. Everybody gets excited in what they call the carnival atmosphere and they forget their basic training.

A man is picked up for possession of marijuana, lollipops, and small toys that could possibly be used to lure children. He says all he wants to do is take their pictures.

Sammy Davis Jr. and Frank Sinatra give a concert to benefit the search. People from all over the country, including prison inmates, send contributions. Most ask that their names not be used. They say it was something personal.

She tells me the police go to a home in Techwood to question a boy about a robbery in the neighborhood. The boy they're looking for was discovered dead four months ago. His mother says it's like a nightmare that keeps starting all over again.

She says she hates me for not being with her. Are you dead Billy? Sometimes I'm just not sure. She wrote that in church, on the back of one of Noreen's offertory cards, with Saint Paul looking down on her, holding his sword and his book. He's the one who first wrote the lines about through a glass darkly, but nobody gives him credit anymore. He meant a mirror, not a window, in case you're wondering. Gus thinks she looks better in windows than she does in real life, dark windows of moving vehicles, cars, trains, buses, planes, it doesn't matter as long as it's going fast enough.

She still dreams about me, too, dreams she's standing in her bedroom looking out the window. I come in and she turns around. She's so happy to see it's me. Then I'm the one at the window, and it's Gus who's coming into the room. She's lying on her bed where bands of moonlight run round and round her body, crossing over her breasts, moving down across her ribcage and back up the other side. When she stretches out her right arm, there's another band that falls over her wrist. Outside the door, the world goes on like it will never stop.

Ray's friend from Burlington is falling in love with her. She doesn't write too much about that, but still, I know. He tells her a story about being on a beach near Ho Chi Minh City and seeing an overturned beetle in the sand, legs in the air, soon to die from the sharpness of the sun. "Sharpness" is the exact word he uses and she likes that. So do I. He saves the beetle, then sees another beetle in the same situation, and saves its life too. Then another, and he saves that one. Soon he is running all over the beach saving these beetles. Finally, he falls down exhausted, gasping for breath. He sees another beetle overturned, and he just can't save it. Behind him, over the coastal hills, he thinks he can hear mortar fire. For a moment he's forgotten where he is. He tells Gus this is pain in nature. Sometimes she knows what he means and sometimes she doesn't.

She tells him my name will still come at her out of the blue and when that happens she has to sit down, wherever she is, like there's a stitch in her side.

Gus has almost perfected her half-gainer. She dives close to a hundred times every night over at Noreen's house, after it gets dark. She keeps the pool lights off to help her concentration. You hear her feet land on the end of the board and the sigh of metal as she pushes off. Then there's a kind of struggle in the air, her body fighting against itself to become hard and cold so it can pierce the water like a needle.

Ray's friend says the judges give that one a ten, just from the sound of it. Gus laughs and steps back up on the board.

It's these moments we're closest, Gus in the air, changing elements. It's always me carrying her out to the end of the board, me letting her go and me diving in after her, to save her if need be.

You know how it is. You've stood there too, mesmerized as evening comes on and all the light drains out of the water, turning it the flat gray of cement, something you can never get to the bottom of. A second later, you'll glance back and the water will have become water again. It stretches itself out, a woman in blue asking to be admired and giving nothing, but nothing, away. You can see yourself floating there all alone, your clothes spread over the water's surface, buoying you up, at least for a time.

185

Elbert & Ross

THEY'S Saturday searches every week now, mostly through the woods in Fulton and Dekalb counties. We goes to 'em but it's easy to forget what you going for and easy to get distracted with hoping you don't find nothing. And then we gets tired. Lately, the girls been coming with us and their pirate-looking friend from up north. We don't take to him right off and we gets to thinking now he's our idea of a suspect, but we don't say nothing about it. Used to be we'd sit down and have us a cigarette and do some talking about what might be in the trunk of his car. Now though we coming to trust him like the girls do.

We talks about dying now too. Got to. Feels like it's all we got left to do in this world. Everybody be thinking about it these days, thinking about dying and them children and now about Buddy Johnson too, but we going to do it pretty quick. We do what we can to put it by, like keep each other's cigarettes hid, but you know dying can't be put by for long. Anyway we too old to quit smoking now.

"Just one," we says, handing over that coffin nail, "and that's all for today. It may as well be a loaded gun I'm handing to you."

"Thanks be and God love you," we says, "He surely do."

Then we coughs both at oncet and a long time to see who going to go first. Whoever coughs longest and deepest, he the winner.

Then the girls'll come to drive us back to Lynwood Park.

"Well if it ain't God's three angels named morning noon and night come to take us home," we says, reaching out our hands.

One of us always want to stay awhile after one of us want to go.

They told us to bring sticks and flashlights, to wear the blaze orange vests if we had one. If you didn't, some folks had orange armbands they was handing out, like mourners wear. That's what struck Mister Joe. We all mourners, he said. In the dark all of a sudden, and don't know where we'll go next.

This Saturday it's a hard piece of ground, ten acres in Fulton County down to Cascade Road between Campbellton and Fulton Industrial. When we gets there at 8:30, two thousand people has already took off into the woods. One old nigger was saying how he going to bring his chainsaw along in case anybody has to be cut out of something. He just looking to be prepared. Other folks has hedge clippers and rakes. They told us to be sure to shine our lights down into hollow tree trunks, sift our hands along the bed of Camp Creek where it run shallow. We supposed to be on the lookout for patches of cloth, fresh digging in the ground, and stacked-up rocks. You could watch folks walk off into the woods and then fan out like they was dancers. There's something beautiful and kind of ghostly about it, and for all of us in the woods, it was mostly silent. Nobody talks much. Nobody come to talk, except about anything that looked like it could be a trail or a clue. So it's right quiet.

We all decides to split up, even Ray and his girl. Mister Joe he hover around us all for a while, but then he go his own way too. He the only one who slogged all the way into the creek bed, and down into the water to feel his way along the bottom. It was some powerful sight from high up on the banks where we was, like to be watching John the Baptist. He'd stand up then bend down into the water, over and over, moving right down the middle of that creek, bending and raising up, baptizing invisible saints. We starts noticing a lot of the crowd stop what they was doing to watch him alone down there in the water. Mens mostly, and then they foreheads would wrinkle up and faces get cloudy before they goes on with they own work searching.

When somebody find that skull and them small bones, there ain't the fuss you might expect, just a quiet message traveling back into the woods, and it was more like sadness than feeling we was doing anything good. The police come and close off the area six feet in every direction, the height of an average man, Mister Joe said, and there was a break in his voice. Folks comes to stand at the ropes, holding them in they fists for a while, then they moves back into the trees. We got to watching them, and every single one, mens, womens, and children old enough to understand, they all shaking they heads. Some of the mens swear, but they voices raise no louder than air or the sound of your feets moving over the grass. Some in the crowd fell to whispering names of the children it might be. When we read it in the paper, we recall how a young gal down front of us went to put her arm around the waist of the lady beside her and said the name *Angela*. Joe say that mean of the angels, like he don't think we know.

After the police come Joe take hisself back down to the creekbed and we move along in the same direction we was going in before, not too close but keeping him in sight. We don't want to be left alone in these woods, not even with good-hearted strangers. The girls and Ray's gone somewheres back of us and we think we hears they voices, but after seeing the police digging and kneeling over that pit in the ground where them bones was, we don't trust ourself to know nothing for sure. We hearing child's voices calling everywhere and bones crunching under our feets. Close by the water in the shade, we feels a chill come on us where the sun be mostly blocked out by pitch pines. It feel like we passing into another season.

We watch a man come half walking half sliding down the side of the hill toward the creek where Mister Joe is. He's a big man with a powerful air to him, black like most of the searchers and wearing a green armband that's right garish beside his orange vest. He gots an intent look about him, purposeful. It's all in the way he come on down that hill, like gravity is the least of his worries.

He stop hisself right at the edge of the water and call out to Mister Joe.

"Can I talk with you a minute?" he say. The water carry his voice right up to us, the way water always be carrying sounds that ain't got nothing to do with you.

Joe hold up one hand, nod his head, and wade in to where the man is standing. He keep his feets in the shallows, hidden under water.

"You sir, where you from?"

"Burlington, Vermont," Joe say. "Is there some trouble?"

It's a tiredness in his voice. He can tell what that man's thinking.

"I don't know yet. You out here all by yourself acting kind of funny. This creek's being dragged already, man. The police is a ways behind you. What you going on ahead of them for?"

"I didn't know they were back there," Joe say. "I'll quit then."

That man look off up the creek, acting like he ain't heard Mister Joe talking.

"Is that okay?" Joe call out, trying to catch his eye.

"I don't know, man. I been watching you and I'm going to keep on watching you. I see you bring them kids out here with you and then you ain't even looking after them, going off by yourself and doing work that's already being done. You say you from Vermont? What the hell you doing down here anyway?"

"I'm visiting friends and helping out. I've been reading the papers. This thing tears me up."

"Tears you up? Tears *you* up? What would you know about any of that?"

"I got family like everybody else. Look, if you want me to leave, just say so."

"You got family? Well then go look after them. Where's your family right this minute? Do you know for sure where they is? Because if you don't, if you don't. Shit, man."

Then he stop talking and bend down his head and Mister Joe put out his hand to stop the man's shaking.

"I used to let my boys go out hunting aluminum cans for pocket money. Go everywhere, I said to them, you can find stuff in the strangest places. And they did, too. Then back in March when they was out hunting they found the body of a dead man. That spooked 'em and they didn't want to go out for a while. Then three weeks ago, for some reason it was more important than it had been. The youngest one woke up saying he wanted to go can collecting. He said Momma, we'll find some cans and make some money so you can do the wash. When I think about it, we lost him for a penny can."

"I'm sorry," Joe say, reaching out again for the man's shoulder.

"Look after your own, man. I would of done anything to keep this from happening." He turn away to come on back up the hill.

"I know," Joe say, looking after him up into the sunlight. "I have a father just like you."

They find Buddy like we scared they going to, along by the river clear down to Buzzard Roost Island. Some boys playing down that way run into a sack of trash only it ain't trash, and they say they knowed it right off.

After the service we all come back to work and sit down to dinner back in the kitchen but don't none of us feel like eating. It's an old wound, we say to the girls, to Ray and to Mister Joe, done opened in our hearts and we feeling the pain of it again. We all here wondering how we come to set so much store by hope. It's just a word, we say, and it done took us in, took us for all we was worth. Who going to ask the blessing, we say, and don't nobody answer. We all quiet. Our plates is full of ashes.

Noreen

"IT goes, suffer the little children."

"Noreen," Momma says, looking all of a sudden like nobody I've ever seen before, "I know that part already. What's the rest of it?"

"That's all," I say. "There is no rest of it."

Buddy

I never did like school all that well, and one day after we was outside playing and Miss Tyree she rung that bell, I hid. Then I cut down through the woods, cross the creek and back up to Glenwood Avenue. I took the bus uptown to where my momma was working in Ansley Park and I came walking up the drive through a honeysuckle bush. They got them big front windows and I seen my momma talking on the telephone. I knowed by the look on her face it was school she was talking to.

He's right here, she say, thank the Lord. He just walked in.

Before she even get to ask, I tell her this wasn't my day. Down at school, they kept letting us go outside and hauling us back in again. I can't get used to it.

She say don't never do it again, but most days I did.

Then my daddy left us and didn't nothing seem to go right after that. My momma she know where he is and she say he got him a new girlfriend who 'bout my age. She say she don't give a damn but I know she do. Elijah say he don't neither, then I say it too. That 'bout the only time I done much cussing, when we was all going around talking 'bout them damns we don't give.

I ain't stole nothing won't fit in my pocket or nothing can't one person carry by hisself. Elijah say to keep that in mind when you got to steal.

I ain't lied but about once a week.

I love my momma and my daddy when he come around and even when he don't and Elijah even when he say I can't go with him down to the store.

201

I forgive Ray Gresham for breaking my nose like he did.

It ain't no secrets for me to tell. I ain't had time enough to have no real bad ones.

Elijah

WHEN he get up to the front and they's all standing and singing *There Is a Balm in Gilead*, I sneaks in and crouch down to rest my back against the last bench. I hear the preacher say all them true things about him being a good boy and too good for this world. Then he start to talk trash. He tells us he know what it be like to grow up, how sometimes you believe you ain't never hurt this bad in your whole life and you knows you can't stand to ever again. He say it only going to get worse too, more trouble, more worry, more folks to look out for.

Then he say Buddy is lucky because he won't have to stand this trouble. He been set free, ain't got to ride the long passage through this world to the next. He gone straight on through to joy.

He stop his talk then and it's quiet so deep like to where I guess I could fall into it and drown. I can hear folks weighing his words to find out the heavy truth in them.

"Buddy would of wanted you to believe this," the preacher say like he can read my mind.

That's when I know I got to go or else shout back at him maybe he wouldn't. Maybe Buddy is still scared, off someplace shaking like a leaf, maybe he don't know what all is happening to him. Why is it we always think the minute they dead folks understand everything? I bet they don't and they ain't any smarter than us. If they was, they would give us the one thing all of us wants, and that is for them to come on back and tell us it ain't so bad where they is now.

After that it's like I'm walking in a dream. I ain't living at home no more since Momma done gone back to stay with her momma and I can't stand them two hanging all over me the way they do. I say Momma, I'm fifteen years old and she say the boy gone before Buddy was the same age as me. I stays some with Ross and Elbert but most of the time they talk too much and I can't understand half of it. It's like they don't live in this world.

Sometimes I catch birds and eats 'em when I'm real hungry. I waits till one settle down on the ground then I throws my shirt right down on top of him. Then I build me a fire down in the woods and roast 'em up, way far back near the train tracks or the creek where can't nobody see the fire nor smell them birds.

I generally fall asleep while that fire is burning out, and I think how maybe someday I'm going to catch me one of them birds, a crow most likely, and not roast it up but put him on a string and keep him for myself. I might could teach him to hunt food for me, and I'd feed him and keep him safe and let him fly some so he won't never forget how. It brings me some peace to think on that bird way up in the sky and me attached to him clear at the other end. I watch that bird through the fire going and going in circles, gentle and still and keeping right close to me without hardly a pull at the end of that line. I ain't scairt then until I wakes up and feel my body stiff on the ground and it still be night and I thinks now where is old Buddy and I miss him real bad and then I try to pray. I pray it come a flood or fire to take me up. I pray my momma will come find me and take me on home.

Joe Ithaca

IT would be the darkest hour of the night and I'd hear the sigh of a door opening across the hall, then a slash of dim light where the door to my room opened, and I'd see her move across the window, her body lit up by the moon or the pale color of humid night air, and she'd come to sit on the end of my bed. At first she was so quiet, I thought maybe it was sleepwalking. I'd call her name but she wouldn't say anything, just sit there, straight and tall like she thought I might check her posture. I've known all kinds of sleepwalkers and as long as she wasn't carrying a candle or a knife or a shotgun I didn't worry too much about it.

Then one night after this had been going on for a week or so, she came in and said my name back, just "Joe" and that was all. She reached over and touched my leg down low on the calf where it was sticking out from under the sheet, kind of friendly and reassuring, like she was letting me know she was awake and fully aware of what she was doing. She kept her hand there though, lying still, maybe the rest of the night. I'd doze and wake and that hand would be the first thing I'd feel when I'd come to again, all my conscious self gathered into a three-inch circle fixed under her palm. Near six, the sun started to come up, and about the time you could begin to make out her husband's face in the pictures on the wall, she'd get up and go back to her room.

The next night she starts to talk just like that, out of the dark.

"I try to be sad," she says, her voice rising up at me, "but I'm not, not enough to count. It was getting to where I didn't know him anymore. He was doing something in Tennessee I know because I used to get the credit card bills. Every weekend he'd go with just a sleeping bag and a gun and Sunday night he'd come back, no deer, no birds, just red-eyed and haggard. Wouldn't ever take Ray with him either. I don't know if it was a woman or what, but I know he was drinking. I followed him once, clear to Nashville, caught up to him outside a Stuckey's where he stopped for gas, and even after he told me to quit, I stayed on his course but then I lost him around Clarksville. Just disappeared off the road. I haven't said anything to Noreen and Ray. I don't even know why I'm telling you, except you're a man and you know men, and I didn't want you to think I'd driven him away."

"I never thought that," I tell her, and it's the God's truth.

"I'm glad," she says. "He got to be a mean man, that's all. He wasn't at first. He was sweet. When Noreen was born, he cried into my hair, right there in front of the doctor and God and everybody. But that seems like another life now."

She's quiet and still, her profile cut in a few clean dark lines against the dim light coming in the window. I get the feeling she wants me to say something, so she can hear another voice in the room besides hers.

"What happened to him do you think?"

"I've been trying to decide about that for a long time. It was like he got sick, got a bad cold down deep in his heart and never got well. That's as close as I can get to an answer and even that's not right. I think he's going to end up doing somebody more harm than just leaving them."

"Why?"

"I don't know, but it seems like that's the road he's on."

She turns her head away then, towards the wall. I don't hear anything, but I guess she does, the way mothers will at night, hear it when their kids even dream about moving. Then she gets up and glides out of the room, and I hear her close her door. Sure enough, it's not been two minutes gone by before Ray's standing at the end of the bed looking at me.

"Joe," he says. "You're talking in your sleep."

I roll myself around under the sheet for effect.

"Sorry, Ray."

"It's okay."

The next night she tells me that when her husband's father died last year, the newspaper printed a picture of Willis Gresham next to his own father's obituary. They had the same name and somebody must've mixed up the files. Willis laughed out loud, she says, picked up a book of matches off the sideboard and set fire to the paper right there at the breakfast table. After it was just cinders on his plate, he put his head down on the place mat and cried. She tells me this and then she's quiet for a long time. I think she may have fallen asleep sitting up and then her hand moves to that spot on my leg.

"Joe," she says, "will you hold me?"

Maybe I should have said no, but there's a lot of times a man should say no and he can't. She lies down on her side with her back to me and pulls my arms around her shoulders, working her hips back against my belly. She smells sweet, not sugary, but the turning sweet of compost or sweat. Her skin is cool where it's bare on her arms and shoulders, but warm under her nightgown, and I can feel her breasts moving against my forearm. I feel myself going hard and I wonder if she can feel it too, then she turns to face me and hooks her left arm around my waist, pulling me close.

It's crazy I guess, doing this with the door unlocked and her children sleeping down the hall, but somewhere inside me, down deep, there's a tiny light of a thought burning that says it's all right, a small voice reciting those words about the peace that passeth all understanding.

When it's over she kisses me once on the mouth and rights herself to sit on the edge of the bed. For a while we don't talk, then I feel her twist around to look at me.

"It won't happen again," she says, and I have to admit the first thing I am is sorry.

"But I'm glad about this once," she says.

"So am I," I say.

I see her profile against the window, chin lifted and quivering a little like she's got the scent of something.

"Goodnight, Joe," she says and she's gone.

I lie awake waiting for whatever will come next, but the room stays still and dark and empty until morning.

When I go into the kitchen, she's already there, sitting at the end of the table with her head resting in her open hands. She speaks to me through her fingers.

"Ray's left for Tennessee. He went last night." Her left hand falls to the table and pushes a piece of paper toward me.

"He says he knows where his father is."

For a minute I can't say anything. This is what I drove down here for, but I guess I never thought it would come to pass.

"How'd he find him?"

"Noreen knew. Noreen," she raises her head to look at me, "last night. I think she saw."

Noreen

MALICIOUS Music,

Clarksville, Tennessee. Do not leave money as grace has no price. Do not ignore this.

She's a mustard-colored filly. I remember him saying that. Ugly but she's fast. He told me about her the day before he left. Now you know. You'll leave in the morning.

It could have been something else I saw. In the dark it's hard to tell what with the windows casting in even more shadows from outside. For a second I thought he was Daddy finally come home and a peace shot through me like it was being sent out in arrows from that very bed. Then I heard her say the other name and the air got to be heavy walls of stone pushing in at me from every direction.

Jesus Lord I don't understand what goes on between people. Robbie does and Gus does but it seems too much to give away even if you are going to call it loving. Ray though, he could never have stood it if he knew and that's why I told him about Daddy, to send him away from this house.

Just now I'd like to lay down and die from the weight of these rooms and the strangers who walk the floors at night with their heavy steps and speaking between their bodies languages I can't understand. *By the lips of foreigners will I speak to you and even then you will not listen to me.*

If You speak, Noreen will listen. She will lay awake all night to no other purpose but to hear You. She will get up and put on her clothes and go out and at the failing of Your light she will come back to this house and lay down and listen if only You will speak.

Robbie Lynn

I know this song, but not the name, and I've never heard a lady singing it. I can't think how the people who sing songs like this get through the verses without falling all to pieces and crying their hearts out. Maybe that's what usually happens, and it's only this one time on the record they managed to pull themselves together and get all the way to the last note.

Sam is sleeping beside the Greshams' kitchen table where the linoleum makes a cool hard sheet under him. Mrs. Gresham knows he's there, but she won't say anything about it. Tonight I'm not taking him back to the Whitakers', not tonight or ever.

Outside, Ray and I keep dancing together. He's taken to staring off over my shoulder and when I look up into his face, there's a way to it I don't remember seeing before. We lose track of our steps and move backward, out of each other's hold. He tilts his head to see down to where our feet are still padding in wide boxes and he makes us get back in step. Then his eyes fix in the distance again, past his mother's window where the music's coming from, past her house and yard and out to nowhere I know.

I think how there's times I want him to be somebody else, but I don't know who exactly, not any person I've met before. I want this to be the first dance the two of us, me and not-Ray, have ever had together, the music slow but loud enough around us so we can hide in it and won't need to worry about talk. When the record stops, this won't be the Greshams' house, or Ray, but whoever it is will hold my hand and ask if he should kiss me.

Ray stops dancing and says it's dark enough to light the candles now. It's a surprise for Noreen we've got hidden under the diving board, two grocery bags filled with fifty floating candles each. Noreen's talked about it all summer, how she saw them in a magazine looking like the night sky making a picture of its own self, rising up into the dark like a beacon. She's sick now, Noreen is, sick and thin like she's going to blow away any minute. She never talks unless it's about Jesus. Her daddy is weighing on her soul.

Ray pulls his shirt off over his head and dives into the pool.

"Robbie," he calls out of the water which seems like out of nowhere, "do up some of those candles and float them to me."

I slip off my sandals and sit down with my feet in the water. I turn each candle over until I feel the wick and bring it up with my fingers and then after each one is lit, I set it down in the pool and give it a little push with my toes. Ray swims them out to the middle then to the shallow end then the deep end. I get ahead of him some until there's ten floating candles in a half-circle around my feet.

"What are you tonight?" Ray says, drifting in close. "You're not your regular self."

"I'm a dream," I say.

"A dream?"

"When you dream, this is what it looks like."

I don't know how to explain what I mean any better, so I make my arm swing out to take in the whole pool and the Greshams' back yard, hissing and purring its dark night noises behind us.

I keep on lighting candles and Ray swims away with them. All this time, I'm watching his face, pinkish in the reflected light, his eyes gone serious, blue-black and still. He looks down into each one of the tiny flames like he's never seen anything so wonderful or so strange as a candle that has the power to stay lit in water. I think I've never loved him more or less than I do now.

"What is it, Robbie?" he says.

It came to me in a kind of dream, only I wasn't deep asleep. It was the middle of the night, dipping down into the morning side, and I raised myself up in bed because I thought I heard Momma and Daddy calling in at the window. Outside the whole world was turned sharp and clear with moonlight and at the very moment of my first looking out, I took the moon for more like a skull than the face of any man I'd ever known.

"Nothing."

"I found him, Robbie."

I ask where but he won't tell.

"I'm going in the morning."

I want him to take me with him, me and Sam, but he won't and then I see it's only the body that holds them there with you, the body's deep avenues of blood and muscle leading nowhere but deeper in. They go in hard and you follow more slowly to see how it happens, such a dear calm surprise that your body and their body can do this strange thing and have it be so perfect, you and them the only people in the world who want it this bad, whose parts move like it's what they were born for, whose bodies lie so whitely afterwards along the pure edge of sleep. Remember this always, it's only your body that can hold them. All the rest of it means nothing.

Ray

"YEAH," he says, "that's me. What about it?"

I tell him. He's the smallest man I've ever seen, but still I'm angling to keep my face in shadow so he won't see how beat up I look.

"He ain't here, kid. I told you on the phone."

"I never called you."

"Some girl then. It don't make no difference. He still ain't here."

"But he was here. Where's he gone?"

"Search me. I reckon he's still looking at them walking horses down to Shelbyville."

"Is he coming back?"

"Should do. I got his gear."

"Can I see it?" I say, putting my foot inside the door.

"No sir. I ain't going to be accused of letting no kid run off with his old man's kit bag. You just stay where you are. By the looks of it, you're already in trouble anyway."

He glances down the street.

"You have people with you?"

I tell him I might. I want to put some fear in him, but it could be true too. Noreen and Joe and Robbie Lynn, they all could show up any minute.

"How'd you know I'm his kid?"

"I got eyes same as anybody. You look just like him. He said you might drop in."

"He did?"

225

"Do I look like a man would lie to you? Listen, you give me a little something so's I can go into town and get us some supper, and I'll let you set here a while longer. It's the least you can do."

I step back off the threshold and reach into my pocket for my wallet. Little Richard moves quick as a sly animal, jumping into the clear space between me and the door and slamming it shut behind him. He grins up at me and pats the breast pocket of his shirt, twice, in the rhythm of a heartbeat. I can hear the jingle of keys. I hand him a ten dollar bill.

"You look hungrier than that," he says.

"I'm not," I say.

"Well I am, son. You want to be run off this property yes or no?"

His smallness makes him seem even more dangerous. I pull out another ten and lay it on his tiny palm, across skin that's mottled cream-colored and tan.

"That's better," he says. "Now you stay right out here. Don't try nothing funny like picking locks or going in no windows because I'll be wise to it and won't no place be safe for you after that."

He walks past me towards the yellow station wagon parked beside Joe's Malibu, and his bandy-legged gait makes for slow progress. He moves like both his legs have been broken at one time or another and he had to learn to get along first without one, then without the other, so that now he doesn't know which one to trust. He turns at the car's back fender, smiles, and holds up his right hand, making the thumb and first finger into a gun. He bends the wrist back so the index finger touches his forehead, and slowly arcs his hand over so it's aimed at me. Then he gets in the car, backs it around, and takes off toward town. From where I am, it looks like there's nobody behind the wheel.

I stand still for a minute, wondering if he'll be back. It's twelve miles south into Clarksville and I have a feeling he'll stay awhile. I wonder if I should head down to Shelbyville, but it's a wild idea and I know it.

226

I sit down on the stoop, stretching my legs out and leaning back against the door. The house gives a little under my weight. I bet I could push the whole four walls of it in, but it wouldn't do me any good. He's not here, maybe his gear isn't really here. The dust kicked up by Little Richard's station wagon still hangs in the air and there's a sweet sick smell I hadn't noticed before, like dog shit on your shoes.

From here, you can see straight down the road to where perspective makes the woods close down to a point. It's a bad lookout. You see trouble as soon as it sees you, and there's no place to hide, not in the two unhitched horse trailers or the shed with its door missing. Maybe you could get away on one of the horses. I saw three of them in the pasture beside the lane, a brown, a black with white markings, and the mustard-colored one that must be Malicious Music.

They all three started over to the fence when I slowed down, huge in the sunlight, like they knew who I was. She's a sickening color, that one of his, but she's the biggest and you could see that the other two follow her. Looking at her then, I hated him for not choosing a prettier one, but then I knew why he wanted her. You can't take your eyes off her, her ugliness hits you like a spell or a weapon, her ugliness and her power, muscles and bones knit visible under that sickly yellow skin. It made you go hot and then cold. It was like wanting to be with a girl, down deep in the core of you.

I sit a while longer until I start to notice how fast evening's come on now and it must be near an hour since he left. I try to think how big is Shelbyville, would I have even a prayer of finding him at this horse show. The idea of him getting away from me again makes my heart start to pound so I can hardly hear anything else but the way it's going *lost him again, lost him again.* I hold my hand to it, and then a picture of Robbie Lynn comes into my head out of nowhere, the way her whole body sometimes starts to beating this way, like a working lung or a bird's wing or something else you can't do without. I get to wondering

227

where she is, if she's really left like she said and won't be there when we get home.

There was a time a year ago when she almost drowned. It comes back to me now, how Daddy was throwing quarters in the pool that the girls would dive for. Noreen was there and Gus and Billy Marsh was still alive and Robbie was with them, but she was the only one that wouldn't dive. She lay there stock still and smiled, brown and stretched out on a lounge chair. It made me mad and crazy to see her that way. I wished she could be like other girls and not so far off all the time. I ran over to her and picked up the whole chair and threw it over the side of the pool into the deep end. It sunk hard and she didn't come up blowing water and laughing and slinging her hair back like I thought she would so I went in after her. I saw right away what the trouble was, the hooks on her suit caught in the webbing of the chair. We both tried to get them free, but we couldn't and when she couldn't hold her breath any longer she pushed me away and slid out of her suit, shot up the ladder and out of the pool. When I came up, she was standing there on the cement, her arms at her sides, not even trying to cover herself. We all just looked at her like it was something we'd never seen before, a girl standing naked and still on the cement with the sun just moving off the pool and the woods getting darker and darker behind her. Her body that way made me feel like I was drowning and she'd be the one to save me if only she knew how.

The thought turned into dream snaps me back into this world. I must have fallen asleep and it's getting on towards morning now, and I'm hungry and thinking I might as well go into town too seeing as it makes no difference if he's not coming back, but then a glow begins at the end of the lane and the headlights come up toward me right in my eyes and I'm swearing to myself I'm not going to budge and that car can just come on ahead and drive me backwards through that little man's doorway on into the next world. I'm so tired I wouldn't care.

But it doesn't. He stops the car hard a foot from the toe of my shoe where it's still stretched out in the dirt. He opens the door and slides off the seat, reaching back in for two grocery bags. I hear his laugh before I can see him.

"Sorry," Little Richard says, "sometimes the blocks slip a little on me. Ain't never kilt nobody though. Ain't never maimed nor the like. Ain't never hit no animals. I'm telling you I got a unblemished record, son, so don't you make me no liar."

He walks toward me, and I lean to the left so he can get his key in the door. Even sitting down, I come up to his shoulder. *You could take him out right now*, Billy Marsh's voice in my head says, a voice I haven't heard in a long time. I don't move. There's something in his smallness that makes me think he knows more than he lets on.

"Ontray," he says, and I follow him inside, where it's even darker, only gray patches of light to show where the windows are. Little Richard turns on a lamp by the door and I see the place is no more than a cabin. The walls are hung with tack and pieces of racing silks, yellow and black checkerboard. There's a green recliner pulled up to the front window, behind it a couch covered in burlap except for the chipped wooden arms. On a low table in front of the couch someone's stacked magazines and telephone books. The rest of the room is taken up by a long wooden table, all hacked at and stained with what looks to be blood.

Little Richard dumps one of the grocery bags out on the table. He sets up a loaf of Wonder bread, two blocks of cheese, and a bag of tiny Milky Way bars.

"Help yourself," he says, taking the other bag over to the recliner and settling himself into it. "We'll watch for your daddy. He's bound to be back in a few hours. That show's about over in Shelbyville. In the meantime, we can chat."

He takes a bottle of Johnnie Walker Black out of the bag.

"And I'm much obliged for this, son."

He drinks straight from the bottle in short sips, then leans back and closes his eyes. I break off the cheese in hunks and fold them inside square clouds of bread.

"I ain't going to join you there," he says, pointing at the table, "so eat up. I been having a little trouble with my weight the last three weeks, water retention I guess. Seems like liquids is okay though. Used to could lose seven pounds in an hour sitting in the sweat box or taking them pills. Made you weak though."

"You still ride?"

"Naw, them days is mostly over. I work for the owners. I'm hot walker, groom, and exercise boy all in one, but I still got to be light."

"How'd you find my father?"

He opens one eye and fixes it on me.

"Your father, he found me. We got mutual friends, that's all he ever said, except about his kids. We got to talking one night. He got pictures of all y'all."

Hearing this makes me feel tired. I take the cheese and bread over to the couch where I can see Little Richard from the side and also out the window and down the road.

"Your daddy's a funny one, got a silent way about him, just like you do. From handling animals, you get to know people faster. You get to waiting for other people to reveal theirselves and you come to know their habits in an hour. You and your daddy, it's like being in a room with somebody who ain't there."

He takes two more swallows from the bottle and lets it rest open between his legs.

"Your daddy's got the gift though. He don't ride all that well, but he's got the gift of the long hold. His hands can talk to a horse, feel a horse's mouth through the reins. A horse don't never forget that. Willie Shoemaker has it and he can ride too. That's the mix you want."

"Did he tell you why he wanted a racehorse?"

"He don't have to tell me. I seen it in his face when he come in the door that day. Hell, it was in his voice on the telephone even before that. It's the glamour, partly, and the money-making end of it too, but that ain't all. It's owning a piece of something you can't really own. You can't own one of these gals. You can't even say how they're going to react from one race to the next. But if they win, you get to stand there next to 'em and feel some of that sweat and speed. It takes you out of this world and that's why he done it."

I can feel myself lulled by Little Richard's voice. It comes in a whisper, higher then lower, louder and then soft again. Outside, the sun's beginning to stretch itself in bays of color across the sky, violet and deep red, just color and no light.

"It's pretty," I say nodding toward the window and letting my eyes close.

Things that are too pretty can kill you. It's something Noreen said once, and just now it seems important to remember Noreen and the way she sent me off like I was going for her too, bringing him back for both of us.

When I come awake again, Little Richard's standing beside the couch with my wallet in his hands.

"Hey," I say, grabbing his sleeve. He drops the wallet, stumbles over to the kitchen counter, and opens one of the drawers. I can hear him rummaging through the cutlery.

"I need some cash," he says with his back to me. "Your dad's way behind in his payments."

I think outside myself, like the thoughts are somebody else's, when he turns around with the knife Little Richard will see the pistol and that will scare him off. I don't expect him to laugh, but he does.

"You couldn't shoot me if you wanted to," he says. "You couldn't shoot a living creature, you're so scairt. It's your eyes give you away."

I don't say anything, just hold my aim and try not to shake.

"Come on, boy, you ain't fooling nobody."

I see him down there at the end of the room, but it's like he's not real, not a man but a little talking doll, moving back and forth along the cabinets.

"I want to see my dad's gear."

"It's in the bedroom. You just go in there and see it."

I know it'd be foolish to let him out of my sight and so we stand still like this, caught with our weapons, until I hear a car coming up the lane. I want to look out the window but I make myself fix my eyes on Little Richard.

"That's him," Little Richard says, putting the knife back in the drawer and moving over to the recliner.

I see it now, a light-colored car pulling in beside the cabin. When the door on the driver's side opens, the inside light goes on and he's there, his profile hard and distant, more like the picture I've been carrying than the flesh and blood man in it. Seeing him finally, he gets to be even more lost.

The car door slams shut, his feet crunch across the gravel and then the cabin door swings open. When my eyes shift over to his face, so do my hands.

"Ray," he says, and there's no joy in his voice, only tiredness. "Put that away."

I let my arm drop so the gun runs parallel to my right leg, and he comes to stand in front of me.

"Go home now," he says. "I just talked to your mother. I'll be back next week. You get on home."

I know it's a lie and I tell him so.

"No," he says. "I mean it. We'll pick up where we left off."

He's not smiling. It's a lie, and all of a sudden I see how even if his body's back there, his heart won't be and we'll never be able to pick up where we left off.

"You get on home. I'll be right along in a few days."

It's a lie. I know the only way he'll ever go back now will be in a pine box and for a second I think about how easy it would be to raise my right arm level with his chest and make it turn out that way.

I don't do it. I step around between him and the coffee table and walk to the door, keeping my eyes fixed on Little Richard.

"Ray," Daddy says, reaching out for my shoulder and making his voice go gentle. "Did you see the horse?"

232

"The yellow one? I saw her."

"A beauty, isn't she?"

"I guess." I turn around to look at him, and the question rises out of nowhere. "Why's she called that?"

"Malicious Music? Hell if I know. Names don't seem to mean all that much in this business anyways." Then his voice changes back to how it was when he first came in the door.

"I'll be seeing you, Ray."

It's a lie and he doesn't even know it.

Robbie Lynn

HE said it would surely get me to west Texas, maybe farther, twenty-five miles to the gallon. He said look, it's a black Falcon, and at night no one will be able to see you. I'm going to be Sam's legal guardian in one of these states, maybe Mississippi. They have different laws there. What's yours is yours, and if somebody tries to take it away, you do what you have to.

In Eutaw, Alabama, Sam finally falls asleep. There's a lady deejay on a radio station out of Birmingham, named Jewel. She's eating her supper while she talks, telling all us good folks about a storm coming on up out of the Gulf. By the time I cross the state line west of Cuba, it'll be right on top of us, thunder and lightning, she says, winds going to whip you around by the scruff of your neck and send you back where you come from. Down in Lake Charles there's flooding, train tracks submerged and two day's worth of passengers stranded all along the Gulf. Hard rain and thunderstorms every hour on the hour, masses of electrified air hanging between here and Corpus Christi.

I can picture it. I've heard how in Texas the lightning shoots up from the ground instead of down through the atmosphere. With my eyes closed I could make it happen in my head, streaks of heat and light climbing as high as they can then falling back down under the horizon. These storms turn the sky green, a shade between gray and purple. It's the color of a bellyache, that dull pain you get from eating too much or too little or thinking about things too hard or losing something that belongs to someone else.

Keep talking, Jewel. You've got a lot to tell me about the new world.

I try to picture her, somebody with the name Jewel. She must have the bluest eyes or the greenest, or the blackest, but what kind of Jewel would that be? All I can think of is coal. Her father and mother must have looked at her in her crib and thought they'd never seen anything like those eyes looking up at them out of that sweet face.

Just by the look in his eyes, I knew Ray would find some way to go, knew it all of May, June, July. He has the bluest eyes, and for weeks now they've been staring off past my face, over my shoulder, his vision running ahead of him up some road. Maybe this one I'm on right now. He never would say where his father was, only that he knew and was going after him.

Why, Ray? He won't come back with you.

You just don't get it, do you, Robbie?

No, I guess I must not.

We looked at each other for a while, him at the wheel and me where Sam is now, leaning my head on the window. Then he reached over to touch me and I pulled away.

I'm not going to be here when you get back.

It sounded like talk out of a movie, not like my voice or words I would say. I knew what I wanted then, for the first time. I wanted Ray to say he'd take us with him. I turned my face toward him and waited, my whole body aching toward his, off balance where all the want and need in me gathered on that side. The words got so loud in my head that for a second I thought he'd said them.

Your face catches all the light. The lookout, the pole star. You'll always be here. You'll wait for me.

I left six hours after he did. I only had to wait for it to get dark so I could get Sam the way we always did it.

"It's too scary for me here, right Robbie?" Sam said. "I could get kidnapped like all the other children."

That's right Sam.

238

In the morning we stop at a K-Mart in Tuscaloosa, and I buy him a week's worth of clothes, shorts and shirts, socks and underwear. I buy him pajamas with baseball players running all over them, looking to make unbelievable, lifesaving plays. I buy him a toothbrush and a bag of candy bars to balance things out. He wants coloring books, crayons, and colored paper, but more than anything else he wants maps, a new one every day. He learns the names of the towns as we get close to them, Fosters, Ralph, Marion, Epes, and on to Bonita, Newton, Pulaski, Homewood, and he's sad when we've left each one behind. He draws his own maps of places we haven't been, states that don't exist. He makes ovals of orange with black lines branching out in all directions, whole states of these spider webs, no mountains, no water, just miles and miles of road. He makes fifty pictures and says these are the states he knows. Their names are Mother, Daddy, Noreen, Gus, Mrs. Whitaker, and K-Mart. There's a state called Ray and one called Heaven.

Today is Sam's sixth birthday, or it will be as soon as Jewel makes it midnight over the airwaves.

"Robbie, when was I born?"

"Today, Sam. You know that."

"No, I mean what time?"

I see what he's getting at. Already he knows about exact times and places. It'll make him a good navigator and all at once I'm thinking this trip is the best thing we could have done.

"As I recall, it was a little after midnight." I'm lying but it doesn't matter. You can lie once a week, I figure, without doing anybody harm.

Sam strains forward to get a look in the rearview mirror, to watch himself changing from five to six, and as he sits back, I can see it too, in the dark the round boy's face getting longer and thinner, the jawbone wider and set more carefully, the eyes deeper in the face and more clouded. Then we pass beyond the farthest reaches of this town's lights, Epes is its name, and I can't see anything.

Outside Jackson, Mississippi there's a truckstop with an all-night diner. The lights seem to pulse at us out of the dark.

"Look at that," Sam says, noticing it too. "Let's stop there."

"Are you hungry Sam?"

"I'm six years old hungry," he says.

Inside, you'd think it was another time of day, high noon instead of the middle of the night, the talk is so loud and the light comes at you from everywhere the way strong sunlight does, even though the windows are mostly papered over with truckers' pictures and postcards they've sent from farther on down the line. In the lobby, truckers in cowboy boots talk on the telephone and wander down the aisles of automotive parts and supplies.

The waitress's tag says her name is Lida. Even before he orders breakfast, Sam tells her it's his birthday.

"How old?" she says.

"Six and four hours."

Lida's eyebrows jump up, then she gives me a wise look.

"Careful with 'em when they're thisaway," she says, jerking her thumb back at Sam. "They could turn out either good or bad."

I know what she means and I don't too. I think how this is the beginning of information I'll have to start listening to and storing away for when Sam gets to this certain age or that certain age. I feel a wave of hurt for my parents, for all I never knew about them. How could they have stood it when the lessons come like this, all out of order and from people you don't even know?

We eat scrambled eggs that arrive cut in neat rectangles, sausage, home fries, and toast. I drink cups and cups of burning hot coffee and let Sam have a milkshake.

"It's his birthday after all," Lida says, and I'm deep down relieved to hear she approves.

She brings him a cheese danish with a candle stuck in the middle and starts in on "Happy Birthday." Her voice rises in a cool sweet billow over the whole restaurant and the truckers join in. For a second I think I'm going to cry and I look at the window full of postcards until the feeling passes.

After the singing everybody claps and then in twos and threes the truckers get up and go out to the front, leaving their breakfasts half eaten. They come back with presents for Sam, spark plugs, brake fluid, timing belts, antifreeze, wiper blades, floor mats, a travel mug, road flares, a compass, a United States atlas, a bolo tie, and a Confederate flag. They all say a little bit about how sorry they are to be away from their children or their girlfriend's children or their grandchildren. They want us to forgive them these absences.

When we get up to leave, Lida says our breakfast is paid for and there's a fill-up on the house.

"You send me a card every now and then," she tells Sam, "and I'll put them on the window so we can keep track of you."

We head on to Monroe, Louisiana, to Arcadia and then Shreveport before crossing the Texas line east of Marshall. So far it's rained every day since we left but this morning the sun comes out and it's near ninety degrees. The Falcon's temperature gauge is pushing up toward hot, so I take it slower, heading up back roads in the general direction of Amarillo.

We get to where we like stopping by graveyards to eat lunch or for me to take a nap. They're usually cool and shady and the ground seems to stay damp all day long. Sam climbs on the headstones and looks for names he knows.

I call the Greshams' house from Lake Arrowhead outside Wichita Falls but there's no answer and I'm just as glad because I'm not sure what I would have said to any of them, especially Ray.

I've been having hundreds of conversations with him in my head, times I've said I hate how it always happens the same way, with him leaving and driving to the end of the street where there's a million ways he can turn, north, south, east, or back, and then he's gone. I stand at the window tearing up paper and sailing the scraps after him. The sound they make is a whisper, the cry of his name lost somewhere inside me, or else it's the one question that would make him turn around and come back.

241

We'll haunt each other, me and Ray, there's no other way to say it. We're the kind of ghost that's all body, skin, and real bones, filled up with gravity, bumping into walls and doors instead of passing on through them. We're the kind that can't ever get out of their graves.

Some nights Sam and I will be leaving one town or other, we'll drive past a cemetery and the car's lights flicker blood-red over the gravestones, on and off like the voices of the dead talking to each other in these fits and starts of light. Sam always notices, he loves it so much he wants me to turn the car around so we can pass by again, and sometimes I do.

"What do you think they're saying?" he asks.

"I don't know."

But I do know. It's the same questions they always ask each other. How did it happen? How did you come to be here lying next to me with your eyes wide open?

Tonight at Estelline, Texas, there's one of these graveyards, but this time there's a wreck ahead of us, a fire and then a helicopter taking up the injured. In my head I can hear them, *It's like flying,* they say, *We're not ready,* mistaking copter blades for angels' wings chopping at the stars. I see the car's lights making more talk in the graveyard, see the dead ache for this rising up they now bear witness to. The dead are so much better than we are, the way the dust of their bones billows up when they touch gently, when they cry out, how sweetly they whisper each other's names.

Elbert & Ross

IT come to us in a dream, the way most news do. We dreams it's a horse coming up Cascade Road to Gordon Street and right on into town, clopping along slow without turning his head left or right, just them long black legs swinging out from the knee not stiff but regular like that horse got him a purpose and a destination don't have nothing to do with this world.

Ain't no rider setting up in that saddle, but coming along behind is the missing children, ever last one and they faces is wearing the same look as that horse, like they ain't happy and they ain't unhappy but they gots they thoughts fixed on something we don't know nothing about. And even though they going along behind that horse, you can tell they's giving him his direction. You can see in the air how that horse be paying attention to what come behind him, how he keep his head up listening for the sound of them children's feets.

Along by the side of the road, the mommas stand in a line calling out to the childrens, each one to her own baby, but them children don't answer back, they don't even act like they hearing they mommas' voices at all. They mommas go to calling louder, *Child*, they say, *don't you know your own momma no more?*

We standing off by ourselves at the end of Gordon Street where it come out to Murphy Avenue then on up to Peachtree, and we the last ones that horse and them children going to pass by. It come on and we can't take our eyes from it, casting its shadow over our feets, our legs, up to our faces. And then we seen what make us go to laughing and crying and falling on each other's necks. In the stirrups we seen our own shoes and we looks down to see where our feets is bare. And then we sees that horse is toting our chopping knives and our paring knives and we fall to laughing fit to bust.

Then them children pass by and they turns they faces to us but we can't read pain or joy or nothing. The last one to pass by is Buddy Johnson and he look just like them others, but then he stop and raise his hand like to tell us hidy there you two. Then he act like we s'posed to follow him and we do, stepping off that curb right into Peachtree Street. It feel cold as ice where our feets is bare, but Buddy he turn hisself around to look at us and he say *It ain't far now.*

Gus

"ROSS died tonight," Joe is saying into my ear, his voice gentle over the
phone. "Came home, sat down in front of Wheel of Fortune,
and never got up. Elbert was right there to see him off. Says
Ross got this smile on his face like he'd just met up with an old
friend. Last thing he said was 'There you are.'"

For a while I can't speak, I just hang on to the receiver and
listen to Joe's breathing.

"It's okay, Gus," he says. "You just take it easy. I can wait."

"When's the funeral?" I say.

Behind me, I hear my grandmother stop the clip of her
cards against the formica table. I'm facing away from her, but
still I know how she's sitting with her shoulders thrown back
and her body at attention, staring straight ahead and waiting.

"Saturday evening," Joe says, "at their church in Lynwood
Park. You want to go, don't you?"

I tell him yes and then I can't think of what else to say. I
know the way it goes, the way this kind of news makes everybody seem like strangers.

After I hang up the phone, I walk across the kitchen to
where my grandmother sits with her hands resting over the
cards like she's protecting them. She turns to look up at me but
she won't say anything because she doesn't know what I want
her to do. I come up behind her and put my arms around her
neck and lay my head on her shoulder. I can smell hairspray and
the lavender soap she uses. Her hands rest quietly on one side of
the discard pile, her greasy copy of Hoyle and two halves of an

apple splayed out beside that. Her fingers are thick and strong from years of shuffling cards, playing piano, and lately making things grow in the back yard, but she thinks they're ugly and she wears gloves or keeps them hidden in her pockets. The blue veins twine together on the backs of her hands like rivers on a map, dark where the water investigates the land.

"It's all right," she says when I've told her. "He was an old man, and it was his time. Here, Gus, stay here and help me with this game."

She deals me a hand and offers me half her apple. Ross could make a bird out of an apple. He used to say it was all balance to make the wings. He taught us all how to do it, holding his hand over ours on the paring knife so we could get the feel of the cut.

Saint Peter True Holiness Church was once a liquor store. You can tell from the iron bars still left on all the windows, even though they've been painted white. The building sits close to the street edge in a corner lot, hiding a mass of mud and rocks. Elbert told us the congregation tried to raise money for a parking lot, but they only collected enough for a cement walkway from the front door to the street. He said it doesn't matter anyway since nobody drives to church.

Diagonally across from the Saint Peter True Holiness is the new liquor store and behind that a bar called The Blue Dot. The other two corners are vacant lots. On Sundays people stand around in suits and dresses waiting for the minister to unlock the door. My grandmother and I would drive by on the way to our church and we'd look out at them and they'd look in at us. I wasn't supposed to stare but I did.

Just now, the church is already unlocked. Noreen and I meet across the street and sit for a minute. She's thinner than ever and breathing hard.

"You heard from Ray yet?" I say.

"He's on his way back." That's all she says.

"Did he find him?"

"He found him, but he doesn't think he'll come home just yet." She gets up to walk over to the church and I know better than to ask any more questions.

It's Saturday, getting on toward evening, and it seems like all of Lynwood Park's come out to this corner. Brothers' Liquor and The Blue Dot have their doors open wide. People move between the two or they stand in groups talking and laughing. There's an older girl dancing alone and a bunch of men knit tight together watching her. She stops when we get close and the whole group of them turns to look at us.

The hearse pulls up beside the church and somebody closes the front door of The Blue Dot. Brothers' stays open, but the girl who was dancing calls inside for them to turn down the radio. The street is much quieter now, the music sounding far off and sad. Some heaviness has gone out of the air, and in its place there's our own weight, Noreen's slightness and my heft, white and sharp, forcing its way into the evening.

"Who is it gone on?" a voice asks behind us.

Elbert is waiting for us at the door. His dark suit makes him look younger than he is.

"Ross'd be glad to see you two," he says, leading us inside and down the aisle between the pews. He seats us four rows from the back and tells the people sitting beside Noreen to look after us.

The room is whitewashed and plain. There's not much to tell you this is a church, no pictures, no stained glass or crucifixes, except for a wooden cross hanging up front. The light comes from long fluorescent tubes in the ceiling and the altar is a school cafeteria table with metal legs. Two men stand up in front of the congregation and shake out a white tablecloth to cover it. They light candles and go to their seats.

From the back door a man's voice starts a prayer. *Oh Lord,* he says, the way you do when you're at the end of your rope. The back door closes, the fluorescent overheads go out and we're left in candlelight. The room feels like it's been sunk underwater, the light outside gone blue and cloudy. Voices and music filter in from the street, but there's no tone to them and you can't make out the words.

Even what the minister's saying seems to come from outside his body, or through a long tube. He talks quietly the way you do when there's someone asleep in the next room, a child who probably won't wake up, but could. The minister talks about the vale of tears and heaven. He says Ross is as a little child again. The congregation says amen and Elbert wipes his face with a red kerchief. Noreen is staring down at her fingers where they're tangled together in her lap. She looks far away and lonesome and all of a sudden, I wonder if she might die too and I feel sorry for every mean thing I ever said to her, a little sick with sorriness.

The minister starts to talk about Ross's life, and I listen for a while, but then a beating whiteness starts in on either side of my face. I tell Noreen I need air, walk to the back of the church and throw open the doors.

Saturday evening is a carnival in Lynwood Park. Music rolls out of The Blue Dot in hot waves. People still drift between there and the liquor store, eating their suppers from cartons or paper bags. Just outside Saint Peter True Holiness, four men play dice and next to them, five children have tied the wheels of their bikes together, back wheel to the front wheel of the bike behind and they're riding in a circle, careful to keep a steady pace. They're quiet and serious with concentrating, eyes steady on the wheel they're following.

I sit down on the cement stoop and lean against the church door. The minister is still telling us about Ross's life, how full it was. He says he's found happiness in Ross's time in this world and now in his passage over to the next.

His voice weaves its way in and out of the music coming from The Blue Dot. When Gladys Knight finishes her line of melody, the minister's voice rises to fill the empty space, and when the Pips chant *you know he will*, the minister says those same words about Ross watching over all of us left to carry on.

After the funeral we go to Noreen's house and swim without talking. We don't turn on the pool lights and we don't wear swimsuits. We both do mostly laps because then you don't have to think about whether you want to be on top of the water or underneath it. You can be both.

Then we go to the diving board to practice half gainers. After the first dives, there's applause.

"Very nice, girls."

It's Mrs. Gresham's voice, calling to us from her bedroom window. We hear her pull a chair over and sit down. The house gets quiet again. We wouldn't know she was up there watching except that light from the Hamiltons' next door glitters on the ice in the glass she's holding when she moves it from the windowsill to her lips and back again. Other than this little light, it feels like me and Noreen are the only two people left on the face of the earth and we need each other like we never have before.

After Noreen drops me off, I sit down by the street with my back against a telephone pole, staring up at my grandmother's house through a veil of honeysuckle. A car pulls up behind me, right in beside the neighbors' trash heap. The driver kills the motor and turns out the headlights. I hear a door open then fall back lightly so it doesn't slam. Heavy boots crunch across the gravel driveway.

Joe Ithaca walks past me toward my grandmother's mailbox, opens it, and looks inside. He pulls a long white envelope from his pants pocket and slides it in the box. He stands there a minute, looking off down the street, then he takes the envelope out of the mailbox and starts back toward the car.

"Joe," I say.

"Who's that?"

"It's me, Gus."

I get up from under the bushes and walk toward him. He jams his hands in his pockets and rocks back on his heels, laughing.

"Were you sitting under there all night?" he says. "I've been calling for hours."

Then his arms are open and I'm walking into them. It seems to take forever, as if his chest and belly recede to make more and more room for me. He holds up the white envelope, shows me my name on the front, and tears it into tiny pieces, raining them down into my hair. I ask what it said inside, but he shakes his head and gathers me back into his arms. I want to bury my face in his neck and tell him how strong he is. I don't want to kiss him and then I do. And then I do.

Ray

SO I close the cabin door behind me
with him and Little Richard on the other
side but it isn't sadness or anything like it that hits me then. I
looked at that rented car, the color of puked-back milk, and I'm
thinking okay okay I'll make it even easier for him not to come
back and I walk over to the car and shoot out the tires, one two
three four, one slug into each, which means I still have one left.

When I look up from the last tire, he's standing on the
porch and I can see Little Richard's shadow dancing back and
forth behind his legs.

"My God, Ray, what are you doing?"

I don't have an answer other than what he can see with his
own eyes, so I keep quiet and walk over to the Malibu, thinking
Joe'll be glad to see it back in one piece. When I drive out past
her I think for a second about shooting Malicious Music, but
none of this is her fault. I slow the car and she looks at me out of
her dark kindly eyes and jerks her big head up once like she's trying to say go on, get out of here while you still can and so I do.

What makes me stop an hour later was I thought for sure
it's Elijah Johnson standing there half into the right lane, his
thumb sticking out toward traffic like there's something on the
end of his hand he needs to get rid of. I could have sworn that
it's his exact color and his shoulders and his head going to come
in the passenger window like a bullet. I already have myself
thinking I'll go ahead and give him whatever he asks for, I'm already half telling him that when I notice it isn't him.

257

"You going down near Asheville?" he says.

"Atlanta. But you could ride as far as Signal Mountain. That's still a little out of your way though."

"Some," he says, and gets in the car. "You got you a girl in Atlanta?"

"Yeah," I say. "Why?"

"I got me a girl in Asheville and I bet you and me has the same look on our face."

Then he puts his head back and his breathing evens out. I get this wave of panic over having to ride with a sleeping person without knowing what to call him if I have to wake him up or tell somebody who he is.

"My name's Ray Gresham."

"Skyler Wilson and pleased to ride with you."

Skyler Wilson sleeps for close to an hour, then wakes up south of Nashville where I stop to buy gas I don't really need. If the truth be told, I stopped because I thought it might wake him up, the slamming of car doors and clanking of gas pumps. I was starting to get a little bit lonesome.

"Ain't never been to Atlanta," he says when I get back in the car. "Folks says it's right pretty."

I can't answer him for a few seconds while my breath gets all used up folding my bad shoulder into place over the wheel.

"Collarbone?" he says.

"Yeah."

"Take a fall?"

"No," I say. "Kind of. It was a fight."

Skyler Wilson closes his eyes and shakes his head real slow.

"Man," he says. "I know just how you feel. I got broke up like that in a fight once. It's a man called Ace what done it. Dumbest thing I ever could of done, fighting somebody with a name like that. I truly did think about it at the time, but I went ahead and hit him anyways."

"Sometimes you can't help it," I tell him.

"Ain't that the truth," he says.

I ask him if he lives in Asheville and he says he's about to, going over there now and set to get married to a girl next month.

"She's from Atlanta. Louie Brazil's her name, but I don't expect you'd know her."

"No, I sure don't."

"Still," he says, "with a name like Louie Brazil for a girl, I always got to ask, 'cause if somebody know that name, it surely going to be her."

"You look pretty young to be getting married," I say.

"Seventeen," Skyler Wilson says, "that ain't so young. Anyhow, I worry she going to get away. She's the getting away kind."

I nod and tell him that is a worrisome thing.

"Just now though," he says, "she's right happy where she is. It's a store downtown where you could buy souvenirs of Asheville, shirts and dishrags and them glass bubbles where you turn it over to make snow fall on Mount Pisgah. She likes souvenirs more than any woman alive."

Right then some wish or prayer moves down deep under my lungs and I say to myself I'll take Skyler Wilson all the way home to Asheville, get him there safe and sound back to his Louie Brazil. I tell him that's my new idea and he frowns and says how it's too far out of my way and all, but then he sees my mind's made up. I stop at the next exit to call Noreen, then Robbie Lynn. That's when her grandmother tells me how Robbie's taken Sam and lit out and how they're worried sick about her. She'll call and say *collect from Robbie in Birmingham, collect from Robbie in Jackson, collect from Robbie in Shreveport,* then she hangs up without talking.

"I try to figure her out," her grandma says, "but Lordy, Ray, I can't."

Just after Manchester, Tennessee we split off from I-24, heading more eastward than south, running past the air force base at Tullahoma and Woods Reservoir. There's a state farmers' market there and at this time of day, most of the selling's already been done, having started probably about the time I shot out my daddy's tires back in Clarksville.

The air force planes come in at you out of perfectly empty sky and it gets to where you think maybe you've run across some kind of secret encampment where every few minutes they receive silver messages out of the blue. Across the highway, all the farmers have their backs turned, loading up their trucks. You look at them and it gets to be too much, the feeling that all the secrets of this life are being kept from you, or even that this life is just all secrets and you're never going to be let in on any goddamn one of them. Skyler Wilson talks on about Louie Brazil and how she got that name and after a while I'm thinking of her as Robbie Lynn and Robbie Lynn as her and I know I've got to get back.

When I get home from Asheville, there's a postcard from Robbie saying she's in Amarillo and she'll be coming back but she doesn't know when. I drive past her house every night just to see if the car's in the driveway, a black Falcon Noreen said it was, bought off a boy who delivered the pizza they ordered the night I left. She drove the last two deliveries then dropped him at a bus stop.

Some nights I drive past two or three times to leave a souvenir of myself in the air. I can see why Louie Brazil thinks so highly of souvenirs and when I brought Skyler Wilson into her shop that evening, she said in return for my kindness I could have any souvenir I wanted. I picked out a Cherokee Indian arrowhead belt buckle and a throwing tomahawk for Joe to make up for running off with his car. And I got one of the bubbles with snow inside, not of Asheville but of the Pisgah National Forest with Mount Pisgah in the background, and a forest ranger's tower with a tiny ranger high up in the trees looking out.

In Robbie's neighborhood, the Georgia Power Company is cutting back tree branches away from their lines and there's men up in the trees all over the street, working late into the evening because it's cooler then. I think how much Robbie would like seeing them so far up, how she'd want to watch them for hours, waiting for them to yell down to her all they can see from where they are. She'd watch until her neck ached and her eyes started to water, until she's surrounded by cut branches the men have thrown down. At night from her bedroom window she'll be able to see more of the sky as it wheels by and looks in on her.

For her, I want to be one of those men climbing trees, to read the constellations, tell their stories back down to her and never fall. When she gets back home, I'll say it to her for once and forever.

Joe Ithaca

I tell her the Northern Lights are getting brighter lately and how there's showers of them like fireworks over Lake Champlain every night, storms of light reaching as far south as Texas.

"It's because of the solar flares," I say and she looks up into the sky, expecting a show right over us, but nothing happens. In the bar across the street, they've turned on the strobe light and we watch the dancers' movements become broken and halting. We stay outside even after it's over and when the deejay puts on a slow song, I take her in my arms.

Gus has closed her eyes and turned her face to one side, her cheek resting against the skin where my shirt is open. I like the sight of her with her eyes closed, sleep-dancing in the parking lot. Right before the song ends, she opens her eyes and looks up at me and I stare back down at her. We hold each other this way for what seems like a long time.

I get crazy if I don't know where she is. Crazy like forget to eat and drive to the restaurant, to her grandmother's house, back to the restaurant looking for her. One Sunday morning, I knock on the back door and there's no answer so I lean against the jamb to try and think where to go next and the door's not locked so it opens and there I am standing half in her grandmother's kitchen. I call hello and listen. Way off in the back of the house I hear running water and I follow the sound of it down a hallway. A strange ease passes into my body and I don't hurry but stop and marvel at the pictures on the wall, mostly Gus from babyhood to now, with Noreen and Robbie Lynn, with Santa

Claus, with her grandmother, and set off by itself, Gus as a baby and a woman I take to be her mother, thin with a dark, still face. I don't know whether I should curse this woman or thank her, so I just stand there until the sound of water being turned off and the clank of pipes brings me back to myself.

When I knock on the bathroom door it's Gus's voice that comes back out to me, so I turn the knob and go in. She's there, sitting in her bath, her hair caught up away from her face in a way I've never seen and her skin red and shiny from the heat of the water.

She's surprised but she doesn't say a word. Without thinking I kneel down beside the bathtub and look at her then reach for the soap. Starting with her throat and shoulders, I move the soap in slow circles, down her chest and back, under the water between her legs and down to her feet, bending each leg up toward me then back down again. Next I do her hair and when it's white with soap, I get up and go to the shelf where there's a vase full of jewelry and empty that and use it to dip water out of the bath and rinse her body clean. Neither of us speaks, but if I was going to say anything, I'd try to make her understand that this is my way of honoring her, nothing more. And God knows nothing less.

Then she stands up and I take the towel off its hook on the back of the bathroom door and wrap her up in it. She stays there, up to her calves in bath water, and watching me like she doesn't know who I am. Without saying anything, I turn and walk out of the bathroom, close the door behind me and go to wait for her in the kitchen. I sit down at her grandmother's kitchen table and go through the short list of people I'd be willing to die for. I reevaluate every one.

Noreen

GUS doesn't say anything but I can tell by the way she gets undressed, facing away from me into the mirror. Tonight though, when she turns her back to me it's because I don't know how to explain why I wanted her to spend an hour rooting through these boxes of Momma's old clothes for her cotillion dresses from the summer she was nineteen. That's a year older than we are now, and then there's her wedding dress from the next year in a separate box sealed up tight against time and all eternity.

We each found one with the orchid stem still pinned on the bosom. We do up each other's buttons and stand together in front of the mirror in Momma's bedroom. There's no one home but us and Gus says for once no mommas or grandmommas are waiting up with their sleepy wondering eyes and their books fallen down beside their chairs.

"And it's a damn good thing," she yells at the top of her lungs, "because I feel like a fool."

If I was to put on Momma's dresses would I know how she felt in them and how she feels now? Could I be less Noreen and more her? The point anyways is to be less Noreen. Gus doesn't tell me anything but I know she loves Joe Ithaca and I've known for a long time he loves Gus. And Momma who I know has a good heart has never said a word about that night I saw them. She doesn't even look at him much between going off to work in the morning and coming home and supper and falling asleep. She thanks him for taking care of her children and I look into her eyes while she's talking, but I can't read anything there. I

269

thought if you prayed long enough and hard enough there would be a sense come to the way things are, but I see now it's not. I see now how the lost and the found are in a big pool together swimming to stay afloat and it's too dark to tell which is which.

Gus peels off her dress in a slow striptease, swaying her hips and laughing at herself in the mirror. The corsage pin makes a long scratch on her breast and we run downstairs buck naked and dive into the pool.

"Robbie's in Amarillo," I say.

"I know," Gus says, "but she'll be back."

"Then what?"

"I have no earthly idea," Gus says. "Maybe we could go up north with Ray."

"What about Momma?"

"I know," she says. "I didn't really mean it."

"Yes you did."

Gus keeps quiet. She lets the thought float there in the pool with us like it was Joe in the flesh, waiting silently to see what she's going to do.

Later we find we've locked ourselves out of the house knowing full well those dresses are lying in a tangle on the floor where Momma will see them. We break the kitchen window as quietly as we can.

"It sounds like singing a little," Gus says.

If she was here, Robbie would have said that, and I think Gus wants it to be like she was here.

When I get the broom out of the closet, Gus takes it from me and dances in circles around the kitchen.

"A broom is the best partner," she says. "I don't know why that is. Do you know why that is, Noreen?"

She's still sweeping and dancing when I come downstairs wearing Momma's wedding dress, broken out of its airless wrapping.

"You're going to get in trouble, Noreen," she says.

I go into the dining room to look at myself in the mirror. *When I was a child I spoke as a child. For now we see through a glass darkly but then face to face.*

"Where's your groom?" Gus says, coming to stand behind me. Our reflections look blankly at each other. "Who gives this woman?"

The broken window will give us away and so will these tiny glass stars on the floor, crushed under our feet like fallen heaven.

Gus

HE says he makes up conversations in his head, ones he'll have with his father over the phone, and he wants to practice on me.

"Just say *hello*, that's all you have to do," I tell him.

"I don't want to."

"Just *hello*. And speak up so he can hear you."

Hello, son. How are you?

Pretty good.

How is it down there?

Oh, not all that much better. Kids are still being snatched and nobody seems to be able to figure it out. It's up to sixteen missing now.

If they were white children I bet the police and the rest of them would be working a hell of a lot harder.

Dad.

Mad? Damn right I'm mad, and why not?

So am I.

Well, you let us know what's going on and you stop in to see us on your way back. I don't know why you haven't been here in so long.

Because you were an asshole.

Gradual? Oh, everything's gradual, son.

I don't know what it is got into me this morning thinking I'd take a bath instead. My skin feels dry and tight, tensed up against the weather, against Grandma's voice calling in to say good-bye. She sounds like a stranger and it makes me seem like one to my own self. All these years her being my mother suddenly rush forward and make me feel tired and alone. And it's you too Billy, knowing that a year ago this morning we were out on Lake Lanier.

In the mirror though, surrounded by the gray glow in the bathroom where I've kept the light off, I look almost more beautiful than I ever have and it hits me then *This is the face you'll always have to turn toward the world, this is the whole of all you'll ever do and be, love and make and give birth to.* The words come at me in your lost voice and that makes it even harder to turn away, get into my bath, but I do, still thinking all I ever want is to hear these words the way you would say them. I start to cry, warm water running into warm water.

And just when I think I won't be able to keep quiet, he knocks and walks into the bathroom, Joe Ithaca, whose real name I don't know and feel like I never will even though I think I've always known him. In a flash, I see him the way I just saw myself in the mirror. He is myself walking toward me, my own life kneeling down, one-eyed and strong, in this deep silence.

The word for it is *solemn.* That's the word I hear in I don't know whose voice, how *solemn* to meet yourself like this, to come close to the end of all you know and then see how to keep going.

I close my eyes and feel his hands washing my breasts, my back, legs, arms, my own hands. He empties the vase where my rings are and dips it full of water, water pouring over me, over and over until I don't know what I am, me, him, even you Billy, or just this water, lost in all of them but glad for the first time in my life to be this lost.

Elbert & Ross

WE ain't never been apart before this and it ain't something you gets used to right off. When somebody is gone from you at first you think they coming back and you sits in your chair by the door waiting and saying it won't be long now. Then you gets to thinking up the reasons why they can't come, like it's business to see about or too early in the morning and they ain't waked up yet. After you runs out of them reasons you starts to say it's better they ain't coming today because you don't feel like no company anyhow.

Ray come back from Tennessee and he tell all about finding his daddy and now wishing he ain't never gone looking for him in the first place. He say his daddy call him and his momma and Noreen on the telephone and say when Ray go back up north to school, he going to come visit him but Ray he don't hardly believe it.

Noreen be getting thinner and thinner and she don't never say nothing. She take care of her tables and then she go on home and keep her momma company. If she open her mouth at all she talk about praying or sometimes what she going to do next. She and Miss Augusta, they mentions college some, but you can see how they is like wild fire and ain't going to settle down nowhere and burn low for a while yet.

Folks keep getting off them trains and walking in here like nothing ain't different. They's always asking about the murders and why can't nobody do nothing. We got pictures of each child still missing taped up by the register so everybody got to see them when they goes to pay. It's the last faces they see before getting on the train is the faces of them children. They remembers all the way home.

*What folks has always come in here for is the beauty of it and
they still do. We don't know as they knows that's the reason because
they don't say nothing about it, but it is. We knows most of 'em
thinks they is eating to kill time between trains or do something with
they jaws besides saying good-bye. They ain't tasting any of it but
they's looking at it, so we always did make the plates pretty.*

*It starts out as a lark, way back before any of the troubles, one
slow Saturday when we was both in the kitchen peeling oranges for
the ambrosia salad, having us a race to see who could get the skin off
fastest and all in one piece. When the oranges are gone, we got us
some beets from the sideboard and start shaving away slices then
wrapping them all together to make the petals of a rose. When we got
done, you might have heard a pin drop in that noisy kitchen. The
waitresses is staring, but that ain't nothing new. These waitresses
before Noreen and Augusta was always sweet little white gals who
had that starey eyed way. Couldn't say boo to 'em. Say rump steak
and they'd get red clear up under their pretty straight hairlines.*

*"You gals could of learned this from your niggers if you'd paid
any mind," we say.*

"What is it?" they say back.

*"It's called garde manger." We always did know more than
folks thinks.*

"Gard manjay," they say. "What's that mean?"

*"It means be careful which parts of this you be putting in your
mouth."*

"Do another one for me," one of the waitresses say.

*When it's done, that girl catch it up and hold it to her breast like
a corsage. Sitting like that against the black uniform she wear, it look
like it might be something hurting her. She keep it there until she got
to go back out to her tables, then she fix it up tight in saran wrap and
put it in the icebox. Then they all wants one.*

*Before it's time to start serving supper, we has to take beets off
the menu. You'll get your beets sure enough, but they appear as roses
resting beside the burger or slaw dogs or supper platters. The*

waitresses says they seen you save these roses, wrap 'em up in napkins and take 'em on home.

We can picture it when you gets there. The children or husband
or wife's asking for the love of Jesus why you done brought such a
thing back to New Orleans or Baltimore and you just laugh or you
takes a bite out of that rose flesh and you can't even begin to explain.

Robbie Lynn

"TELL me the story of it again," he says.

It was June 15 and they loved each other very much and so when she said I should go see how Momma's doing in Jonesboro, he said I want to go with you. They each waved to us out the window, their arms and hands making it seem like the car had a pair of skinny wings, but not nearly enough to fly with if they ever had to, which they did. Then they went back to holding each other's hand, his right because he was driving and her left because it was closest.

When they saw her momma, she maybe said you two look so well. I wish I was you and had my whole life ahead of me.

"You're making that part up," he said, mad enough for tears to be coming into his eyes. "Quit doing that, Robbie."

They might have stopped for a milkshake on the way home, or maybe a beer, but if they did it wasn't for long because it was already raining hard. They thought about us waiting at Grandma Wilkins's house and it probably made them hurry some, more than they should have done. The rain was coming down in sheets and splashing onto the windshield like there was somebody running alongside the car slinging buckets of rainwater hard enough to crack the glass and drench their faces. They were on Tara Boulevard, easing over a rise where people say off to the right you can see what remains of the real Tara, and he gave it some gas thinking to get to the top where visibility would be better. It scared him to drive up under the lip of that hill, scared both of them and he reached over for her hand and she said his name.

The driver on the other side was making his first run to Macon and he'd come in off the highway at Jonesboro and he didn't know the road, how just over the top of that rise, it jogs to the left, not much more than this, Sam, from your ankle to your knee. And he may have been falling asleep or tuning the radio or checking the rearview or listening to the slop of rainwater with his head turned toward the back of the truck where the roof leaked.

I have this idea that it was two machines meeting in a long hard kiss of metal, the kind that comes after a fight when you're exhausted and hurting each other has only just turned into something else.

He swerved out of his lane, not seeing their lights until he was right on top of them. People who lived nearby thought what they heard was thunder, but only for a split second before they noticed there was no echo rolling over the hills and no lightning.

Neither one of them was thrown clear or had time to talk or felt any pain. Neither one of them said our names or reached out for the hand of the other. They didn't see their past roll out before their eyes like a movie or hear the voice of God say what have you done with your life.

The people who lived in the two houses on either side of that rise off Tara Boulevard came outside, but none of them farther than ten feet from the front door. None of them carried umbrellas. One man went back inside to call an ambulance and the fire department. The first three passing cars stopped to help and then a policeman came and waved the others on by.

The door on Momma's side had swung open on impact but Daddy had to be pulled out through the window.

"How do you know?" Sam asks.

The man in the truck, he told me everything. He said he didn't even see them.

I pull the Falcon into the Greshams' driveway.

"Where is he now?" Sam asks.

I point over my shoulder behind us and say probably out there, running freight like he used to.

"I bet he hates the rain," Sam says, watching me. "I bet it makes him sorry."

Noreen and Ray are walking toward us down the driveway, faster now as gravity carries them on and opens their arms wide.

"Yes," I say. "I bet it does. Sam, look who's here."

Elijah

"RAY Gresham," I says and he don't say nothing back, just stop walking in the middle of his driveway. I come out from under the honeysuckle and tell him it's a truce between us.

"That's good, Elijah," he say and then he keep watching me like there is something else we got to do now.

"You ain't been here Ray," I says. "I mean I ain't seen you all the time like I used to."

"I've been gone a few days," he say, "but not all that long."

"Is that right?"

"Are you hungry, Elijah?"

"Hungry? Why you think I'd be hungry?"

"Well last I heard from Buddy, you weren't staying at home and I just thought maybe you might be."

"No Ray, I ain't hungry. I guess I gots to get along now."

I see it have to be me that do the turning away. This is Ray Gresham's driveway and he can stay in it as long as he want to but I can't.

"Elijah," Ray say when I got one shoulder aimed toward the street, "you should go on back to work for Elbert. He needs you. You know Ross died."

"He did? When?"

"A week ago. They could use you right now."

"Elbert won't stay long without Ross there too," I says.

"No I don't guess he will."

"Then they's going to have to shut down, ain't they?"

Ray nods his head.

291

"And then I have to go back up north," he say.

"You got to do what?"

"Vermont," he say, "I go to school in Vermont."

I says is that right and then I takes a step back and ask him if he found his daddy yet. Ray nods his head and I knows from his look I ain't supposed to ask no more questions, but I can't help myself and I says when is he coming back.

"Never," he tell me and stand there watching my face. "You sure you're not hungry?" he say after a while.

"Naw, I got to get on."

"All right," he say. "I'll be seeing you. Go talk to Elbert."

When I stops at the bottom of the driveway, I sees how I don't hate Ray Gresham at all no more and it make me sad. When I used to spend all them hours laying for him in these bushes I liked it, them days going by with people's feets passing up and down and waiting for Ray like I was iron and he was a magnet drawing me out.

I ain't hungry but I should of gone up and eat something like he said because walking down this street now it feel like doing what can't be undone, it feel like I ain't never going to see Ray Gresham again, and the thought of it all the sudden like to knock me down right here. I can see up ahead where Peachtree cross the end of his street on the hilltop and it's hot with the cars and buses and the air shining full of heat that rise up off the road in silver waves. On Ray's street there's trees to keep off the sun and bushes to keep watch in. Up on Peachtree there ain't no cover or shade or nothing.

I quits walking and stands facing the street lights starting to come on up ahead. Then I feels a grip like Buddy's hand used to get on my arm and it make me close my eyes. It's a car coming from behind so I get out of the road and wait for it, hoping the driver ain't already seen me and is fixing to stop. But he don't stop, he just swerve in close so I feel a heave of air to almost make me fall into the street, but it be like that sweet hand on my arm take ahold of me and keep me steady on the grass.

Right then it make me think of the one time Momma took us to Six Flags last summer and me and Buddy have to go on the rides by ourself because Momma is too scared. We get on the roller coaster and on the last turn, Buddy say he want to touch the wheels on that car we was riding in and look to see if it come right off the track the way people say it do. When we gets to that turn, Buddy go to grip my arm and lean way out. He see the sparks coming off them wheels and he shout my name, *Elijah, Elijah, we on fire*, but we ain't scared and them tears in our eyes is from the wind rushing at us and they don't mean nothing.

When that car turn off onto Peachtree, I turn too and walk back to Ray Gresham's house, all the way up his driveway, alongside the honeysuckle in his neighbor's yard closer to the house than I ever come before. I reach to the carport and climb up the stone wall beside it up onto the roof and down into the boxwood on the other side. From right here I got me a clear view of the swimming pool where they is all in the water, moving like to make you think that water is full of ghostly fish.

What I do now is keep watch, making sure it ain't no harm come to anybody here. Harm can come so fast and so quiet and they can't hide from it, not with them shiny white bodies. It be like they got candles held to they faces and they be down in the water shouting here I am, can't you see me? Folks like that need somebody to watch over them because they got one foot in the grave already. I ain't watched over Buddy hard enough, but now I knows more of how to do it.

And maybe tomorrow when Ray Gresham come outside first thing in the morning, I might rise up and tell him what I been doing for him out here all night long and I might say now Ray, now I am most hungry.

Noreen

BEING alone in a swimming pool at night is like being alone in church. There's that same feeling of somebody keeping you company, only they're invisible. You're not though, you're all body, all flesh and blood pounding in your ears, heavy and sinking fast. You count on the invisible to save you but you don't know if it will. The light in church is watery too, full of old tears, blue and rheumy like an old man's eyes after a lifetime of crying.

It struck me tonight, who does God love more, animals or us? He baptizes us but wild animals get baptized every time it rains and fish every second of their lives, if you think about it that way.

Everyone else has gone inside, Ray and Robbie Lynn with their arms around each other, telling their stories in fits and starts. Momma is here tonight too, listening for the first time to how Ray shot out the tires on Daddy's rented car. She smiles, shakes her head and says *Oh Ray* without knowing whether to be glad about those tires or sorry. Then she asks about the horse, Delicious Music she says, and from then on that becomes her name. Joe laughs loudest of any of us and puts his arm around Momma's shoulders and I feel a little sadness for them.

Gus comes out of the kitchen door where the window's been fixed and sits down on the side of the pool with her legs dangling in the water.

"Noreen," she says. "Don't worry."

"About what?"

"About who's going to go where," she says. "Nobody's going to go anywhere just yet."

"But it's August already," I say.

"Don't I know it," Gus says.

"Ray has to start school soon," I tell her.

Robbie Lynn stands framed in the light pouring out the back door.

"He isn't going back," she says, sitting down beside Gus, "and Joe's going to stay for a while too."

I wish the others would come back outside too, Momma and Ray and Joe Ithaca. I think I'd like for us all to be in the water together, to start from the water, then walk to the steps and rise out of the shallow end and start from there, open the kitchen door, go into the house and start from there too.

I say it seems like people have got unfinished business. Robbie to take care of Sam, us at the Brookwood, at least until they find a new cook to help Elbert. There's another search through the woods this Saturday and we promised to go. Somewhere outside this pool there's Elijah and all those missing children to be found. It's August now and so heat lightning shatters the air every night and shows how little of this world is at rest.

BESIDE the pool the girls take off
their dresses and set down the flowers they've
been carrying, which aren't flowers at all but thin slices of potato cut
and twisted together to make the petals of a white rose. In the dark,
you can't see how they've wilted and gone brown at the edges, so if
you'd seen these girls coming up the driveway, you might have thought
they were carrying empty white bowls, holding them out from their
bodies as if they're fragile or dangerous.

They step out of the dresses, leaving them heaped on the cement in
three pools of glowing phosphor. Emptied this way, the dresses look evil
or poisonous and the girls can smell the scent of their own bodies rising
out of the fabric. The water touching their skin is cool from rainfall ear-
lier in the day, making the flesh feel like it's shrinking around the bones.

Noreen spreads her hands over the surface of the water. She can
hear the other two moving ahead of her into the deep end, and when she
turns to follow, her forearm brushes along something moist and oily,
cold as ice. She cries out that it's a snake and springs half out of the
water toward the side of the pool

And she's right. Sometimes it happens that a king snake or even a
water moccasin gets turned around in its ancient path through this world
and mistakes somebody's swimming pool for the lake or river that used
to be there.

299

"What did you say?" Gus calls from under the diving board, but Noreen is already at the light switches, chopping upward with her right hand, her body turned back to look.

Gus freezes like a deer caught in a car's headlamps but Robbie Lynn keeps swimming past the snake that's come into this pool to die. Noreen walks down the steps at the shallow end, moving closer to where the dark form floats half out of the strainer. In the white lights the three girls' naked bodies look otherworldly, pale opalescent beams cutting through the water the way fire cuts through ice. They make a circle two feet from the snake, then Robbie Lynn reaches a hand out to touch its middle.

"I don't know why I did that," she says. "It's dead though."

"We can get it with the skimmer," Noreen says.

The moccasin coils itself quietly in the skimmer basket and Noreen lifts it out of the water and carries it over to the trash can. Gus and Robbie Lynn walk up the steps in the shallow end and follow her.

"Should we shoot it or something?" Gus says. "What if it's just stunned?"

"It's not stunned," Noreen says back. She puts the lid on the trash can, moves to turn off the pool lights, and they're all three blinded again, the way you get after lightning makes everything clear as daytime. They walk like sleepers or the wounded with their arms held out, find the shallow end and sit down on the step with their feet in the pool. Slowly they ease their legs in, testing the water, feeling its surface. Then they're swimming again, all three bodies lean and slick with darkness.

In bed tonight you'll lift your arms out from under the sheet and try to hold your hands over your eyes to feel the fingers' coolness and blot out the memory of light, but you can't. You can't find your own hands in the dark until you're pressing them to your eyes, making sparks that dip and whirl like perfect dancers. The howl of the Southern Crescent comes fierce and long, longer than you remember it being, but when it's gone the night settles back into itself, waiting for the answer daylight might be. Outside your bedroom window the very *last of the rain is seeping upward to become the morning's haze and the sound it makes is soft and steady, a voice calling, a hissing out of the peach trees.*

Acknowledgments

I would like to thank Kathryn Lang and Freddie Jane Goff for their work on the manuscript and the Corporation of Yaddo for its support. Thanks also to George Haupt for permission to use *The Hill* by his mother, Shirley Eliason, and to Philip and Frances Levine for their generosity.

Rocky Thies

About the Author

Liza Wieland was born in Chicago and grew up in Atlanta. She earned the B.A. degree in English from Harvard College and the M.A. and Ph.D. in English from Columbia University and has worked and taught in New York, Utah, Pennsylvania, and Colorado. A recipient of the Radcliffe Prize for Poetry (1981), she was a Yaddo Fellow in Writing in 1988.

Her short story "The Columbus School for Girls," first published in the *Georgia Review* (Fall, 1991), was selected for reprinting as the lead story in *Pushcart Prize XVII: Best of the Small Presses* (1992-93 edition). She is currently working on a novel and a collection of short fiction in addition to teaching American literature and creative writing at California State University, Fresno. *The Names of the Lost* is her first novel.